BABY ME

SAVAGE VIPERS MC
BOOK 4

ANNE STORM

Cover Design © Christine Michelle
ISBN: 979-8-89706-012-2

READER CONTENT WARNING

Anne Storm books are not for the faint of heart.

They might contain "triggers" for mental health and are not for "safe readers".

XO,
Anne Storm
Potential triggers include: Infant cancer
Foul language
Violence
Stalking
Murder
Arson
Mental health issues
Sex between the hero and the heroine
Sex between other people

Nudity described on page

Author's Note:

If you have not done so, you might want to read Surprise Me (book 3 in the Savage Vipers MC Series) before starting this book. It gives the background between Tripp, June, and Kim from when they were younger. While it is important for the this story moving forward, Baby Me can be read without the addition of Surprise Me, but I highly suggest reading them both.

For obvious reasons, this book starts before Wait for Me (book 1 in the series).

Tripp and Davina's daughter, Coral, has Infant Acute Myeloid Leukemia (AML – see info about this at the back of the book). There are certain fictional treatment options that were written in, and prognosis that might be uncommon in reality, but serve to create a happier ending for this book's purposes.

ABOUT THE BOOK

Davina
*I walked away from the club the minute those two pink lines
showed up on the test. There were only a few good options for a
baby daddy among the club's men, and the odds weren't in my
favor that my daughter's father was one of them. So, I never told
them. Until I had to. Her life was on the line and my secret might
just destroy the happy little life I'd managed to find. Especially,
when it turned out the baby's father was the President of the
Savage Vipers MC.*

Tripp
*I married my kids' mom after a one-night stand led to her getting
knocked up with my son. Despite leaving my high school
sweetheart behind for her, we had a good life until she was killed.
Eight months ago, I reconnected with my high school sweetheart
and when I finally got around to bringing her around my kids,
history repeated itself. Our former club girl had a baby. She was*

sick and needed help. That little girl also turned out to be my daughter. Her mother was a woman I had been interested in but couldn't have because of our age differences and the fact that she was a club girl. Despite all that, she quickly became the one woman I couldn't let go.

PROLOGUE 1

KIM

May 1st

A KNOT of tension sat heavy in my stomach all day.

At first, I thought maybe it was to do with the kids, since they were both out doing their own thing. Then, I wondered if Tripp was okay.

> KIM: Weird feeling all day. You good?

A few minutes later his reply came with a photo of himself and Mack working on a Harley in the garage.

> TRIPP: All good here, babe. You need me to come home?

> KIM: No. Probably just about to start my period or something.

I knew the excuse was me trying to blow off the twisty feeling I had in my gut since there didn't seem to be a feasible cause. Still, it would keep him from rushing home or worrying.

> TRIPP: Thanks for the head's up. I'll bring chocolate and rum when I head home later.

"Something doesn't feel right," I mumbled to myself after reading his last text. In an effort to take my mind off the horrible feeling, I sat down in front of my laptop and started going through the pictures I'd taken of Star and her friend, Ashlynn, the other day. The little divas thought they were both the next up-and-coming models and popped poses that made my eyes roll. Still, it had been fun to play around with them, especially since my baby girl would officially be a teenager in just one week.

It was difficult to think about where the time had gone. Kip had just turned fifteen in March and already asked his dad for an upgrade to the dirt bikes he rode on our property. It wouldn't be much longer before our kids would be full grown. Tripp had been promising me a vacation around the world once they were out of the house, and I planned on holding him to his promise.

Every time I pictured the two of us trapsing around the globe it made me chuckle to think of how differently we'd look by then. We still had at least eight years before it was possible, and my old man was already going gray in the beard. It was early for him to have gray hair, but apparently it was genetic happenstance to gray early in his family. I'd say poor Kip, but the silver fox look never seemed to go out of style. My boy would probably end up rocking it early like his dad.

Over our mantel hung a picture I'd taken at Sturgis three years earlier. Mack had stayed home with the kids because he was still doing physical therapy for his leg. An exhausted trucker fell asleep at the wheel and nearly took him out. My brother's quick thinking and perfect reflexes were the only reason he came away with a broken leg instead of being hit head-on by the eighteen-wheeler.

Still, as much as I wanted to hurt people for how over-worked and over-tired truck drivers always were, thanks to a broken system and time/pay imbalances, the near tragedy allowed us that perfect week together. The picture was one some club girl took for me while using my camera. The girl was long gone from the club, but the picture remained a favorite memory. Tripp and I stood in a small circular patch of trampled down grass surrounded by motorcycles.

The way he looked at me always felt like seeing complete and utter devotion in print and the smile on my face never failed to make my heart flutter with the memory of that moment. I felt the most pure, honest, love for Tripp when that picture was taken, and it came through loud and clear in the print. It had been the first time in years we were able to get away together and it was sorely needed at the time.

That week brought us closer after months of us drifting a bit. Marriage was never easy. Despite the love we had for our children, they made it even more difficult as we lost time with one another to manage the kids' schedules. We didn't have real problems. No one was stepping out, our finances were fine, we were just missing each other and in doing so, managed to push a little further away after every disappointment.

That week in Sturgis was a tipping point, one where we vowed to take more time for one another. It was just as important to dedicate those moments to ourselves, for our children, as it was to be there for them. Without that balance, we drifted. In the three years since, we managed to make our relationship a priority again and we'd never been happier as a result.

The anxiety that was eating me up inside didn't abate as I took that walk down memory lane. Instead, it increased as the day moved on. Tripp would be home soon, and then I'd tell him about my little run-in with his ex-girlfriend this morning. Honestly, seeing her earlier in the day was probably the reason for my anxiousness.

I'd taken some photos to the newspaper, and on the way out, I accidentally bumped into someone. When I looked up, the woman seemed familiar, but her garish red locks and pursed-face stare didn't register at first.

"You!" The woman growled at me. I took a step back, so that I had room to maneuver because the threat of violence in her voice couldn't be mistaken for anything else.

"You still haven't gotten what's coming to you after all these years, have you? I would have thought Tripp would have buried your ass in a swamp somewhere by now, but I guess your brother is still protecting you."

I glared at the hateful woman, and it still wasn't clicking until the woman beside her laughed. "Damn, the red hair must be throwin' her, June. She has no clue who you are."

The other woman, a blonde and far better looking, if life

4

hadn't aged her so harshly, had finally clued me in as to who the hell was standing in the lobby of the newspaper talking shit about me.

June fucking Hargrove, Tripp's ex-girlfriend from high school.

"You're really brave standing here threatening me, especially when I didn't even recognize who the fuck you were. That's how little you mean to us. We don't think about you, sweetheart. Don't concern ourselves with your whereabouts and what have you. You do not register on our radar at all. You haven't since the day Tripp kissed you in the Piggly Wiggly parking lot and realized it didn't even compare to what he had with me.

"And honey, if I'm being honest, one of the club whores would have been better than you for that man. Poor guy didn't even know what it felt like when a woman had a real orgasm because you were so grossed out by sex. Now that I think about it, he did complain about you once. It was when he told me that you couldn't take the full length of him without complaining and making him back out again. Sad, really, that you thought your pathetic ass could keep a man when you didn't give or receive oral, and then couldn't even take a dick by your own idiotic request." I looked at her friend then, "My old man is a God when it comes to oral," I explained. "She was missing out."

Despite wanting to rip her over-processed red hair out at the roots, I walked away after that leaving them both gaping and speechless. The smile on my face was indication enough of the satisfaction I'd received from our little encounter. No one could blame her for still being hung up on Tripp. He was a catch, and unfortunately for June, she'd fumbled her chance with him. As I'd stated, she hadn't been all that satis-factory in the bedroom department because she was a prude.

Looking at who her parents were, there was no doubt she came by that honestly, but still, you would think the woman would be over the man who was so far out of her league she hadn't realized it, even then. She always thought she was the better half of them when they were coupled up, simply because her family came from wealth. The bitch had been wrong, and she'd lost the best man in the world as a result.

I wouldn't cry for her loss because it was definitely my gain. Tripp and I had been happily married for a long time and we had two beautiful children to show for it. Our son might have been conceived accidentally, but our daughter had been planned.

Like I said, we'd been happy since he chose to devote himself to me and not her. There was never a day when I doubted his love for me and the feelings in my heart for my old man only grew with each day we spent together.

My family was my everything.

By the time I got back home, after running all my errands, that impending doom feeling started to set in. It had nothing to do with being insecure where June was concerned. There was just something in the air beyond the thick, humid heat that seemed to suck the energy right out of me. It was almost always warm in South Georgia, but it had been exceptionally, and unseasonably so, all day. I'd been sweating like a whore in church by the time I got into the house.

I glanced back up at the photograph of my old man

smiling down at me just as I heard glass shatter in the kitchen. There wasn't even time for me to take two steps in that direction to see what caused the noise before something connected hard with my head and I went down in a sea of blackness. The last image I processed was a swath of crude red impeding my vision of the picture I'd been staring at moments ago.

PROLOGUE 2
JUNE

May 7th

TRIPP LOOKED EVEN MORE handsome than when we used to date. He put my sorry excuse of an unwanted husband to shame. I wished that I could go over and wrap my arms around his body and let him know that I could be the shoulder for him to cry on.

It wasn't time for that, though. That bitch only died a week ago. It should have been years ago, but they were careful with her in the beginning, especially when the kids were younger.

The kids.

Those little brats were the reason I couldn't approach him yet. Tripp never cared about that bitch. He fucked her out of duty after she drunkenly took advantage of him that time while I was in Europe. I don't know how he was able to forgive her for that, and I imagined it had to do with the little cunt being his club brother's sister. Still, I wasn't stupid.

I would have to bide my time and pretend to live a happy little life with my clueless, lump of a husband that my parents picked for me. He wouldn't even be in the picture if it wasn't for my father's stupid rules. I couldn't inherit his bank, but so long as I was married to a man that he approved of, that man could inherit ownership with some hefty stipulations that protected me.

I did everything he ever asked of me. I left Tripp alone, despite the fact that I knew I could have gotten him back. I went to college, double majored in business and finance, and could run the bank he started better than my father ever could. Still, he wouldn't leave the business to me.

I yanked at my hair as I watched my future husband throw a rose down on the man-stealing whore's coffin. Then I smiled because she might have stolen my man temporarily, but she got what was coming to her in the end. I wasn't even sure why they bothered with a whole coffin when there couldn't have been much left of her, considering she burned up in a fire. It was just a shame that their kids hadn't been with her when it happened.

They were the reason why I had to wait even longer to claim the man who belonged to me all along. I needed them gone. Otherwise, they might put up a fuss, and I wasn't stupid enough to believe Tripp would choose me over his children. I thought that might have been the case once, but he proved me wrong. I would bide my time, wait for the youngest brat – another whore-in-the-making like her mother – to grow up and move out, then I'd swoop in, and Tripp would be mine forever.

CHAPTER 1

TRIPP - 8 YEARS, 9 MONTHS LATER

"Tripp Martin, is that you?" A woman called out to me from across the parking lot. I'd pulled in to check on my Harley Breakout. The damn thing kept choking out when I put it in fifth gear. I pulled my attention off my bike problems and glanced around until I noticed her. Recognition was immediate.

"June?"

She grinned widely as she walked toward me with a very deliberate sway of her hips. "I thought that was you. I noticed from my office window."

I glanced at the building, only just then noticing that I was sitting right in front of the bank her father owned. Since she worked there, I assumed he still owned the thing. It figured that she ended up working for him.

"How have you been?" I took her in from top to toe for the first time and realized that she had done a fantastic job maintaining her figure after all these years. Time wore on her face a little, but it was barely noticeable under the makeup she had on. She didn't seem to have any grays in her hair, unlike me, though that could have been down to a good hair stylist on her part. In fact, since it was still blonde, it must have been down to the stylist she used. I'd nearly forgotten that she'd once been a brunette.

Truth be told, I hadn't thought about June at all in years. Once Kip came along, and things changed to seal the bond between Kim and me, anyone else faded out of existence for a while. When we came up to breathe from our brand-new little family, my focus remained on Kim, Kip, and the club.

"I've been doing well. Obviously, I ended up working at my dad's bank after college."

"Where did you end up going to college?"

June looked hurt before she was able to school her features. "You really don't know?"

I shook my head. "By the time you graduated, I had a son to take care of. Didn't really keep up with much of anything except when to change diapers and feed him."

Her eyes narrowed on me for a minute in what almost looked like a menacing glare before once again smoothing out. "Isn't that what his mother was supposed to do?"

I chuckled and kicked back against my Harley. "Shit, June. She had to sleep sometime. We took turns taking care of our kids."

I wanted to feel bad, considering the hurt in her eyes at the mention of me having more than one child with Kim, but I didn't. I loved my wife and the life we made together, that included both our children. There would never be a day where I apologized for it.

"I heard you had a girl, too."

"We did. Kip and Star. They're well, Kip is in the club with me, and Star is off living her adventure, but she's doing great."

"Your son still lives with you?"

"Nah. We're in the club together. He lives at the club-house now."

"Wow!" Her eyes turned down to the asphalt beneath our feet. "That has to be weird sharing space with your adult son, considering the things all the men in the club get up to together."

"Nah. No different than living in a house together. We stay out of one another's way unless we don't want to."

I knew what she was insinuating – that maybe we had seen one another have sex with the club women. That was never my style and Kip wasn't one for public displays either. Besides, he was secretly dating Scout. I almost chuckled thinking about how they thought no one was the wiser. She was a club girl who no other man dared to touch because they all saw what was going on between them. If my son didn't claim her soon, we'd have to have a talk about her position in the club. It wasn't fair to the other girls that Scout was living at the clubhouse and earning the same as them and only had to be available to one brother.

"Kip is a good man. I'm thinking he'll be settling down with a woman of his own soon. As for Star, she's living out an adventure. I hope she comes home and claims the man she wanted before, since he's someone I wouldn't mind her settling with now that he grew up, but we'll see." I shrugged and continued to smile because one of the greatest joys in my life was talking about my kids.

"I know this is going to be hard for you to grasp, but it still hurts to hear you talk about a child you had with another woman. That was supposed to be us."

I pointed to the gold band on her finger. "Looks like you weren't waiting around all this time."

She glared down at the thing. "This is business," she stated as she held the hand with the ring on her finger up and showed it off with disdain clear on her face. "My father wouldn't allow me to inherit the bank unless I married a man he approved of. I have a marriage of convenience only. The truth is that I did wait for you," she laughed darkly, as if it hurt her to make the sound. "I always thought you'd get tired of doing the right thing and get rid of her."

"I loved my wife," I growled the words at June, ready to walk away from her juvenile, jealous bullshit again.

"Stop. That was 'younger me' and her hopes I was speaking of. As I grew up, I knew that you must have grown fond of her, otherwise you wouldn't have had another child. That was when I started dating again. After hearing about your daughter being born, there was no hope left that you would come back to me."

We stood there in silence for a bit with June lost to her own memories and me to mine.

I missed Kim every damn day – even now. I'd been with other women since she passed away, but none ever compared to seeing her wake up with that beautiful smile on her face, ready for another adventure with our family. Fuck! I needed to get my mind off her before I started bawling like a baby in the bank's fucking parking lot.

"I'm guessing you're the boss, so you won't get fired for

being out here so long. Still, it looks like someone is trying to track you down." I tipped my head toward the bank and watched as June's face blanched then turned grim before she spun to face me again.

"Maybe we can get together and have lunch or dinner sometime and catch up."

"You're married," I reminded her.

"Your marriage meant something to you, but mine is just a way to keep the family business in the family. Besides, I just want to catch up with an old friend. We spent nearly four years together and you were my first everything, surely that warrants at least a little time to catch up as adults?"

"Sure," I agreed somewhat reluctantly. Curiosity about her marriage arrangement was getting the better of me because I never thought June would stoop to following her father's orders down the aisle. When she handed her cell over to me, I plugged my number in and then texted myself as a reminder that it was June's number.

"I need to get this hunk of junk back to the garage. It's been problematic."

"It's sexy," June said as she walked slowly back toward the bank. "Like its owner."

The last little added bit had my ego flexing after being dormant for quite some time. Shit, the last woman I'd been interested in was Davina, one of our club girls. I chuckled to myself as I thought about what I'd almost done. It was just a week or so ago that I thought about asking her out on a damn date. A club girl who was more than a decade younger than me. I shook my head at the thought. It was bad enough my son had taken one of the girls off the market without making it official. There was no way that I could do the same. And there sure as fuck was no way I could date her while she came back to the club and gave it up to my brothers.

The fact remained that Davina seemed too sweet to be a club whore and there was something about her that reminded me of my deceased wife. Not in looks. Kim had been all dark hair and curves for days. Davina was tall, naturally blonde, and her blue eyes sucked me into them every time I looked her way. Davina was quiet where Kim had been bold and boisterous. There was something underneath it all though. Maybe it was her struggles when she was younger, the same ones that led her to a life with our club, that made me see her differently.

I could feel the strength that brewed underneath the quiet surface. Because of that, I'd almost asked her to be mine alone. That lasted all of a minute until I remembered how fucking young she was. If Star came home and found me with a chick who was only slightly older than her and her brother, she'd skin me alive before taking off again.

Davina was a dream I had to give up on before it ever started. It was the reason I'd never fucked her. My dumbass reasons didn't stop me from wishing I had though. I glanced back to watch June as she swayed those hips all the way back to the man who had come out of the bank to look for her. As soon as she got close, she threw up a hand as if to tell him to stay out of her business. The man glared back at me before following June into the bank.

We couldn't start anything while she was married, but catching up with June, having my ego stroked by someone else, might just be enough to take my mind off the woman I decided I couldn't have.

There was the little obstacle of June being married, but it felt like my kids might accept her before they'd accept me being with a younger woman who worked for the club. I was going to accept June's invitation to catch up and see where it led us.

I wouldn't have given up my time with Kim for anything, but maybe June and I were meant to be together after all. We had nearly four good years when we were younger, before everything happened that fateful summer to change it all. Maybe, now that we were older, the same obstacles that were in our way before wouldn't be there.

Then again, she was married this time, and that felt like a huge obstacle. Whether it was a marriage of convenience or not, it didn't bode well to start things off on the wrong foot. Instead, I'd just go to that dinner with her to catch up and see where things went from there. If we reconnected in a romantic way, I'd make sure her marriage was over first before we went there.

A sick feeling settled in my stomach for a minute at the thought of reconnecting, possibly romantically, with June. My thoughts turned to Kim and what she would think about it. My wife would have wanted me to move on, probably long before now, but there was that niggling sensation in my gut that told me she would not approve if that woman I moved on with was June. There was just too much history there, and not all of it was pretty.

What would the kids think if they knew the full history? Would they welcome June, so long as she didn't make disparaging remarks about their mother? Would June be okay around them, or would it hurt her too much to see the proof of the life I led without her? She had a loveless marriage. Mine had been something to cherish, and one I missed with all my heart. I couldn't help but feel like she would be resentful of the life I'd led.

CHAPTER 2
TRIPP - 3 MONTHS LATER

I SAT at the bar in the clubhouse and stared down at the phone in my hand.

> June: Sorry, not feeling well. I need to cancel our plans for the night.

Well shit. There went the rest of my night. I set my water on the bar and started typing back.

> Tripp: Anything I can do? Bring you soup? Shit, I guess that would be awkward since you still live with Barry, huh?

I sent the message even as I shook my head about how sick it made me to do so. Fuck. How did I wind up mixed up with a woman who was married? I swore to myself after the way Kim and I got together that I would never start another relationship with anyone in such a messy way.

The only thing that helped in this situation was that June was obviously in an arranged marriage and we had an agreement that we were just friends for now until she could wrestle the bank out of her dad's grasp when he retired. Despite June's many attempts and hints, I wouldn't be intimate with her until she was divorced, and she knew that. Until then, our plan was to be friends, get to know one another again – as adults.

> June: Sorry. I'll make it up to you when I'm feeling better.

> Tripp: Ok, darlin'. Take care of yourself. If you need anything just call.

"Hey man, you have mystery plans tonight?" I glanced up to see Breakneck standing there.

"Nah, plans just canceled."

"You gonna tell me about these plans you keep having? Seems to be serious or headed that way and you know we have to vet anyone brought in, especially as an old lady."

"It ain't there, brother. If it gets there, I'll let you know. Until then, I'd appreciate you keeping quiet. It's not something I want in the open."

"Fair enough. Wanna ride?"

"You mean your night doesn't consist of wearing out all the club girls again?" I teased.

"Nah, not feeling it tonight. I need the ride instead, been feeling cagey."

"Let's go." I agreed and jumped up to join my club brother.

"Feel up to heading into Augusta tonight?"

"Yeah, man, that sounds like just the thing. It's been a while since I rode anywhere beyond town limits."

Breakneck nodded, because of course he already knew that shit.

"Kip worried about me?" I finally asked because this impromptu ride seemed a little too convenient.

Breakneck grinned at me. "Maybe, but I honestly needed the ride and time away too."

"You have a thing for Scout?" I asked, wondering if my son hijacking one of the club girls for himself was hitting our boys a little harder than I originally thought it would.

"She's a fun piece, but nah. That's all your boy. If he's smart, he'll lock her down before someone doesn't give her a choice in having to fuck them."

"If someone doesn't give her a choice, they're going to answer to me."

"You know what I mean. She can't exactly turn a brother down if Kip doesn't man up and claim her. We have our brothers coming in from Kentucky next week. You gonna tell them she's off limits?"

"Nope," I shook my head. "He has to claim her, or she has to walk away from the club. Those are the only two reasons she won't be an available body at the party because that's part of her contract with us."

"Fair warning, brother." He huffed out a half-laugh. "I don't see that shit ending well for them."

"I guess we'll see. He's either going to claim her or have to let her go because my boy isn't one for sharing what he considers his."

"Truer words..." Breakneck let that sentiment hover as he put his lid on and started his Harley.

We rode right into the heart of Augusta before Breakneck turned onto Center Street. I groaned because it was obvious that he had a destination in mind. Meanwhile, I thought we'd just get to Augusta, fuel up, and head back. Breakneck obviously had a bigger plan in mind for the night. I hoped he didn't bring me out here to get drunk at a bar and hook up with anyone.

June and I might not be officially dating yet, since she was still married to her husband, but we were serious enough that I wouldn't do that without discussing the dynamics of our arrangement first. Knowing June, she wouldn't agree to us being free to explore other people until her divorce. Then again, it had been three months since we first went out to 'catch up' and there wasn't even a whisper of when said divorce might happen.

She kept putting me off by saying that her father needed to hand over the reins to the bank first, and once he did, she could file the day after the ink was dry.

We pulled up outside of the Chop House, a pricey restaurant that did not at all look like it was open to bikers as its clientele. It certainly didn't look like a place Breakneck would willingly dine. Still, he parked across the street from the place, and I followed suit. The minute the engines were killed, I started to pull my helmet off, but Break stopped me.

"Leave it on. Wanted you to see something. Wasn't sure it was going to be worth the site until I heard your plans got canceled earlier."

"What's that supposed to mean?"

"It means," he stated coolly as he pointed across the street, "you need to keep your helmet on so you aren't noticed and can watch what's happening in the outdoor seating area over there."

I turned to look and after scanning the outdoor area once, I took it slower on the second pass and noticed a familiar woman walking back to a table in the middle. She leaned in and kissed a man who pulled her chair out for her and then sat down with a wide smile on her face. My phone pinged with a text, and I took it out to look while I wrapped my head around that shit.

Breakneck, who had been thinking with his fucking head instead of being shocked by the sight, had sent me a picture of that kiss and her smile.

Fucking June. The woman who claimed her marriage was a convenience only and that she was getting divorced soon, sure did seem very pleased to be out on a date with her husband and their friends.

"How did you know?" I asked my club brother.

"You've been spending a lot of time with her. Found out she was married, but it seemed like you knew that, so I wanted to check out the details. Didn't seem she was on the up-and-up with you. Would have let it go because if you want to do married broads, that's your shit to deal with. When you said your plans were canceled, I guessed you didn't get the real reason for that. If you knew about this, then we'll forget it ever happened and ride back to the club-house for a beer."

I nodded my head. "'Preciate ya, brother." I threw a leg back over my bike and sat there for a minute. "She told me she wasn't feeling well. Know she's married. It's complicated as she's an old flame from before Kim."

"Figured there was history," Breakneck said.

"Don't want this getting back to my kids."

"My lips are sealed. Free advice, Prez." He said and when I didn't stop him, he carried on. "Married bitches are more trouble than they're worth. History or not."

"Seems like it," I stated as I turned to look back at the table again. June was leaned in with her arm around her husband as she used her other hand to wipe something from his mouth. Then, she leaned in further and kissed him again for everyone to see. I started my Harley and backed it out of the spot I'd pulled into. As I waited for Breakneck to do the same, on the road in front of the restaurant, I revved my engine loudly. It caused a bit of a stir as everyone who was dining in the outdoor area glanced over. I knew the minute June clocked me because I was watching her.

My full-face helmet didn't give it away that it was me, but I saw her stiffen all the same, especially when she noticed my club brother with me. He was still backing out, thanks to a kid who ran behind his bike who he had to wait for. She could clearly see the Savage Vipers patch on his cut from where she was seated.

"Yeah, June. Caught ya." I murmured into my helmet. I had no right to be mad. She was married and I knew that going in. Still, it felt like she had grossly misrepresented herself and the relationship she had with her husband. The only thing I could think was that this was all some elaborate plan to fuck with me because of the way I chose another woman over her all those years ago. If that was the case, then fuck that bitch. I hope she enjoyed her revenge. She wouldn't get any more of a reaction out of me than she already had.

I felt my phone buzzing with text messages the whole way back to the clubhouse. Fuck her and any excuses she had for me. I was too fucking old to play these kinds of games with women. That was one of the reasons Davina hadn't been a realistic option. Game playing went hand in hand with most club girls and younger women. Not that I'd ever heard of her being involved in bullshit drama, but still. It was a concern I'd had. It was one that I didn't think would be a worry with June, despite her relationship status, because she was old enough to know better.

Served me right for thinking there was an age limit on bullshit drama.

When we finally got back to the clubhouse, Breakneck hesitated before going in. "You good, Prez?"

"Yeah, man. Thanks for that little trip. It was enlightening."

"Not even gonna bust my chops for digging into your business?"

"Nah. You were doing your job. The results of you lookin' out for me and the club aren't your fault. Head on in and enjoy the rest of your night. I'll be along in a minute."

"I can save one of the girls for you," Breakneck called out as he made his way to the door. He didn't wait for my answer.

I wouldn't be touching any of the club girls tonight. Something I'd learned about myself long ago was that whenever life through a curveball my way, it was imperative to take a moment to process that shit before making any snap judgements or decisions.

Despite my fingers itching to pull my phone out and check the messages she left me, I waited. The night air felt like a thick cloak around me until a sweet voice spoke up from the shadows.

"You look as though the world is on your shoulders and you only just now realized how heavy that is."

I turned to see Davina leaning against the wall, lingering in the shadows cast by a tree that needed trimming a couple years ago and no one had gotten to it yet.

"Getting my mind right about a few things," I answered as she stepped out into the beam of the security light Break-neck and I had triggered when we pulled up. "What are you doing out here alone?" Davina shrugged, which forced her wavy blond locks back off her shoulders to drape down her back. Swear to all that is holy, the woman looked like an angel in that light. Her blue eyes sparkled as she cocked her head to the side and really took me in.

"It almost looks like someone broke your heart."

"Not my heart. Someone broke my trust, though."

"For some people, it's the same thing."

"Nah, those people never had their heart involved if it feels like the same thing," I countered.

"Is there anything I can do to make your night better?" Her question came off in a bashful and more concerned way rather than alluring and full of innuendo. The latter was how any of the other club girls would have sounded. I shook my head because one thing I wasn't going to do was use sweet Vina as a release while my mind was on another woman.

"I appreciate the offer, but I have some business to deal with tonight. Why don't you take the night off and give your-self a break, though. If anyone gives you a hard time about it, tell them to come see me."

"It's not necessary. I know my place here."

"Your place here isn't conditional on you never having a minute to yourself, sweetheart. Take the night and do what-ever you want. Read a book, get some extra sleep, or what-ever it is you enjoy."

Her eyes lit up when I mentioned reading a book, so I assumed that was something she enjoyed. It made me smile because I remembered a time when a book was the best gift I could bring someone.

"What do you like to read?" I asked as I got to the door of the clubhouse.

"Anything with a good story and a happy ending," she admitted shyly. I could almost see the blush that bloomed on her cheeks, even though it was too dark for it to be real.

"Good to know. Have a nice night, Vina."

"You too, Prez."

By the time I got inside, the office no longer appealed as a destination, so I grabbed a couple long neck bottles of beer and headed back to my room. I downed a beer, took a shower, got comfortable, and sat in my chair with the other beer and my phone before I bothered to read the messages that flooded my phone on the way home from Augusta.

June: I know that was you.

June: Please, pick up. It wasn't what it looked like.

June: Okay, so you're probably headed back to Danville and can't look at these messages yet. Please, call me when you get in. At least text me to let me know you got there safely.

June: I'm worried about you. You should have been back by now.

June: Seriously, Tripp, it isn't what it looked like. That couple work with my parents and we had to keep up pretenses.

That was the message I decided to reply to.

Tripp: You could have been keeping up pretenses all night long and it wouldn't have bothered me. Fact is, you lied about where you were and why tonight. You could have just been honest about a dinner with business associates, and all would have been good.

June: Says the stalker who followed me.

Tripp: I didn't follow you. Went on a ride with a club brother to Augusta after you cancelled. What were the odds that I'd see you in a fucking restaurant in Augusta when I thought you were home sick? The lies are the problem, June. They'll always be a problem for me.

June: I'll be back in about an hour. Let's meet and talk.

Tripp: No need.

I powered off my cell. There was a landline in my room in case someone needed to get in touch for an emergency. There were also plenty of assholes in the club who could come get me if I was needed. I sucked back the rest of the second beer and then went to climb in bed. I snagged the book I'd been reading the night before and smiled at the thought that maybe Davina was similarly curled up in bed with whatever held her interest.

My eyes inadvertently scanned to the other side of the bed, the one that remained empty, and a longing to fill that spot hit me down to my soul. I was man enough to admit to myself that I was fucking lonely. After having Kim as my partner in life so long, it had been more than difficult to adjust to all the small things where she was missed. Having that person beside you at night to decompress with – even if we're doing our own things – was one of the moments I missed more than I ever thought possible. My mind tracked back to a certain blonde beauty who was probably reading another page of her book at that moment. I allowed myself a minute to indulge in the fantasy of having her here, snuggled into my side as we both read our own books. Fuck.

I rubbed the center of my chest where it hurt in the best way to imagine it. If only she was something I could have permanently. The crazy thing was, I couldn't picture the same peaceful moment with June in a similar scene. She was never one to enjoy a good story, unless it was of the gossip variety. She also wasn't one to just soak in the peace of a moment. Everything had to be go – go – go with her. Some-how, I didn't think that had changed much.

CHAPTER 3
TRIPP

JUNE TRIED to contact me numerous times over the next two weeks, including getting up the nerve to call the clubhouse looking for me. That was the only time I responded to her.

> Tripp: Do not call my clubhouse again.

> June: Please, Tripp. This is ridiculous. I wish you'd let me explain. It really isn't what you were thinking. Barry even said he'd be willing to talk to you to clear things up.

I couldn't believe this bitch thought that me talking to her husband would help the situation. Her husband being the key words there. What kind of fucked up situation had I gotten myself into?

"Fuck!" I groaned. The club was preparing for a big Halloween bash coming up and I didn't want any part of their happy, holiday bullshit. Honestly, I just wanted to drown myself in the bottom of a bottle whenever I thought about what a mess I'd made of shit by falling back into things with June. I should have known better. Some people don't change. We weren't compatible back in the day, and it was exceedingly clear from her persistent messages and calls that we were still not meant to be.

I was fed up with the bullshit and lost in dreams of the peace I used to come home to when Kim was still alive. "Need a fucking drink," I said to my empty room before I headed out to the bar to go grab a bottle to bring back. It wouldn't be beer, though. A stronger bottle was the only thing that could quiet my thoughts and discontent.

I grabbed a bottle from behind the bar and was about to head directly back to my room when I felt as if someone's eyes were focused on me. I turned to see Vina staring at me from across the room. Without any thought at all, I crooked a finger at her in invitation. She hopped up and moved across the space as if being reeled in by an invisible hook.

"You okay with this?"

"Of course."

She nodded before I quietly guided her back to my room.

"Last chance to back out." I turned to look at Vina as we reached the door to my bedroom.

"Why on earth would I do that?"

I shrugged. "Never had you back here before." It was an admission I didn't want to make. There were plenty of times my fantasies played out with Davina following me back or me bringing her to my room. She gave me an odd look, as if it was a common occurrence that I had other women back here instead of her. That wasn't the case, and maybe I hadn't phrased that well enough, but before the night was over, I would prove to her just how special it was that she got an invite into my private domain. Years ago, when I first took another woman, it was a club girl, one who was no longer with the club. She never made it to my room either. None of them had over the years. Not that there had been many times that I went there. Normally, if I picked up, it was a couple towns over so my exploits wouldn't be thrown in my kids' faces.

I let all those thoughts go as we walked into my room, and I shut the door behind us. The minute I had the lock engaged, Davina turned and ran her hands up my arms and over my shoulders until she pushed her fingers into the hair at the back of my head and scraped her nails across my scalp. I threw my head back, so it was lower, and she could reach more of it.

"Feels really good, sweetheart."

"Why don't you make yourself comfortable and let me take care of you. You're always so tense with the weight of the club on your shoulders. Let me make it better for you tonight."

"How are you planning on doing that, Vina?"

"I'm going to start out with giving you the best damn massage you ever had. We need to work out all this muscle tension and once your body is feeling good and loose, I'll help you work out your other frustrations any way you choose."

"Your first priority is taking care of me and making sure I'm not riddled with tension?"

"Yes."

"Is that something you do for all my brothers?" Fuck, I

regretted asking the question the minute the words left my mouth.

"No, it's not. You look like you need it though."

"It's not required."

Her slight shrug and the sweet smile she gave me made me want to turn the tables and pamper her ass instead. "It was just an offer. You're free to say, 'No,'".

Like fuck that was going to happen. I removed my cut and then pulled my shirt off without saying a word to her. After I put them on my desk, I leaned down to take my boots off and then everything else I was wearing.

I nearly lost my focus when Davina began to strip her clothes away. When she was down to just her panties and bra, she moved further away until she ducked out of sight into my bathroom.

"You have any lotion, oil, or lubricant in here?" she called her question out without leaving the room.

"Medicine cabinet."

As I waited for Vina to come back, I laid face down on my bed with my head tipped to the side so I could watch the beautiful woman as she confidently sauntered her mostly naked self to me.

"I'm going to start with your neck and shoulders because that is where your muscles look like they're nothing but hard knots."

Vina gently traced her fingers up my spine and sent a pleasant chill to spread across my whole body.

"You have to take better care of yourself, Tripp. This is kind of ridiculous."

"Not every day someone offers to give me a massage around here." I smiled at her.

"Well, consider it an open invitation. If you need to relax, I don't mind helping you out."

"I'll keep that in mind." I knew it wasn't done on purpose, but the woman was planting ideas in my fucking head. Ideas of this being a nightly thing. Maybe every other night, we would swap, and I'd give her the massage before we turned in and read a book until we fell asleep. That would have to be after I fucked her sweet pussy, though. I honestly wasn't sure if I would make it through the massage she wanted to give me without turning over and taking her, considering she had been a long-time fantasy of mine that I refused to indulge in before.

As she massaged my scalp again with her fingertips, my lizard brain decided I should ask her to marry me, so that we could have this every night. Thankfully, my common sense prevailed, and I remembered that wasn't a possibility I could entertain for many reasons.

Davina spent nearly an hour working the kinks out of my muscles from my neck down to my thighs. By the time she scraped a nail gently over my balls for the fourth time as she worked on my thighs, I was finally done.

"Sweetheart, as much as I love your hands on me like that, because they're fuckin' magic, I think it's about time I showed my appreciation."

"I didn't do this for what I could get in return."

"Didn't say you did, Vina. Now come over here." I tapped the top of my chest to indicate where I wanted her perched. "Get up here and let me show you how to relax, too."

She wiggled up from where she'd been straddling the backs of my knees until she hovered above my chest. I helped move her so that she was held up just above my face. Her panty-covered pussy was a thing of beauty. Once again, I found myself reluctant to unwrap the present that was so close I could almost taste her in the air. She smelled delicious. More importantly, she smelled incredibly turned on.

I yanked the silky, soaked fabric to the side and flattened my tongue out as I licked from her hole to her clit in one smooth movement. I took my time, savoring my first taste of the woman I'd had hundreds of times in my dreams but never in real life.

"Why does that feel so good?" she moaned as I started to devour her pussy.

After Vina came all over my face, I flipped her over onto her back on the bed and quickly pulled her bra and panties off her body. Seeing her like that, all blissed out from orgasm and melting into my sheets turned me into a madman. I slid up her body and sank deep in her pussy before it even registered what I was doing.

"Perfection," I groaned as her tight heat wrapped all around my cock. The flutter of her inner walls damn near sent me over the edge. It was then I realized I was in her without protection, but it would have taken an act of the fucking gods to get me to pull out and suit up after feeling like I'd just landed in heaven.

"Fuck, you feel so damn good, sweetheart."

"Tripp. God. So good." Her words were lost to my shoulder as I started to pick up my pace and rocked my body into hers even harder. Then, she shocked the shit out of me and started meeting my thrusts with her own.

"Yes, baby. Fuck me back!"

Each time she pushed up against me it drove my cock into her wet heat harder until I felt like I was about to come apart. She hadn't gotten off again yet, so that couldn't happen.

I flipped us again and told my blonde beauty to ride me. Her blue eyes sparkled with intensity as she stared into my own. I told her something about wanting to see her tits sway while she bounced on my dick, but I couldn't take my eyes off the burning blue orbs staring down at me. I could almost feel the difference. The heat was there, the challenge of chasing an orgasm, but there was more. With Vina, there had always been more between us. It had been the reason I'd never gone there with her and now that I had...

Her inner muscles clenched down on my cock, released, and clenched again as she rode me, taking me out of those thoughts and into the moment again.

"Fuck, baby, you keep doing that and I'm going to blow my load before you get off again."

"You keep doing that and I'll get off again before you do," she promised with a teasing lilt to her voice. "I'm..." Before she could say another word, I tugged both her nipples at once and rammed myself up inside her as she slammed down onto me. Vina screamed out her release and the sensation was enough to take me with her. I blew my load inside the woman I'd been fantasizing about for more than a year and had zero regrets in doing it. She didn't mention our lack of protection, so I chose to stay silent about it too.

When she collapsed down on my chest, I rubbed her back and leaned forward to kiss the top of her head. She had her ear to my chest, listening to my rapid heartbeat as it slowly worked its way back down to a normal beat. When I felt her relax into me even further, I asked if she was all right.

"Mhm, just basking in the afterglow. I can move," she tacked on as if she was suddenly afraid she might be making me uncomfortable. Fuck that. When she flinched, as if to do just that, I put a stop to it.

"Don't want you to move. Stay like this, unless you're ready to leave."

"Not in a hurry to be anywhere else."

"Good." I slid sideways and took her with me. She started to turn away and I helped until she was spooned into me with her back against my chest. I wrapped my arms around her, afraid if I drifted off she would disappear and I'd wake to this having been the best dream of her yet, but just a dream all the same.

It wasn't a dream though.

We talked about where we saw our futures going and my sweet, beautiful Vina wanted nothing more than a family to call her own. It made my chest ache that she obviously longed for something she hadn't experienced and simultane-ously made me want to be that for her. She wanted children though, and my two were both grown adults. The thought of starting over didn't scare me the way it probably should have. I'd had mine when I was still young and there was plenty of time to do it all again before I was too fucking old to enjoy time with a new family.

Before my thoughts on the matter got too deep, I took my

angel again. I made love to her the way I thought she deserved. I made love to her to show her how I felt when there was little hope of taking it further. It wasn't fair to either of us. There were just so many obstacles that it fucked with my head, especially after she fell asleep in my arms again when we were finished.

I dozed for a bit, but when I woke with Vina still in my arms, the panic set in. What if me hooking up with a younger woman was the thing that kept my daughter from coming back home? Could I sacrifice the family I had now for the one I wanted? Would that even be something I had to do? It didn't matter because the fact that the possibility existed meant that I had to nip this in the bud. Vin wanted a family and I already had one that I'd fucked up enough. This couldn't be the thing that kept my daughter from coming back into the fold because it would make me resent Vina down the road and that wasn't fair to her.

Fuck.

Then there was Kip.

He was with Scout, but he hadn't always been. What if he had fucked Vina too? How would that look to have a stepmom he... Irrational anger swamped me at the thought. Fuck. There was no way I could introduce a woman as a potential stepmom to my adult kids if one of them might have been inside her already. I shook the thought off because it seriously made me want to punch the fuck out of my boy. This was why it would never work between Vina and me. I hated it, but there was no denying the complications we faced.

Instead of facing them with her, I chose the fucking

coward's way out. I got up, dressed, and quietly left the room with her still sleeping in peaceful ignorance over the choice I was making. This would be our one time together. Maybe, after our talk, she would figure out what she wanted in life and go out there and find her own happiness.

I rubbed at my chest where an ache built at the thought of her creating that family she wanted without me. It was for the best, though. She deserved far better than a widowed bastard in charge of a bunch of dumbass bikers who had zero qualms about using a precious gem like her and tossing her out.

I was the current dumbass who did it.

My phone beeped with an incoming text. I pulled it out without thought and the message that waited for me was jolting. Not in what it said, but because I'd completely forgotten about the sender.

> June: Please, I'm begging you to come hear me out. We had a chance at something and I'm not going to let you run from that.

Little did June know, I was running from the chance I really wanted to take, but she wasn't the woman I wanted to take it with.

CHAPTER 4

DAVINA - 2 MONTHS LATER

"No, no, no!"

The stupid test had to be wrong. I grabbed the next one and looked at the results.

"No, dammit!" I yelled again at the stupid stick. There was no use in denying it. That was the third one today, the sixth since I took the first test yesterday. The first had been a fluke, or so I thought. The test had come from under the bathroom sink, where one of the other club girls left what remained of a combo pack. When that was positive, I went to the store and bought five more. I took two more that same day.

Then, because I was too stubborn to accept the truth, I took the other three this morning when I woke up. The tests stated that first morning pee was the most accurate. I thought there was still a chance that the others had been wrong. Unfortunately, six positive tests were hard to dispute.

"I can't believe I'm pregnant," I mumbled to myself. Then I glanced around the dingy bathroom, as if seeing the space for the first time. It hadn't been scrubbed clean – truly clean – in ages. The once white grout had turned black in spots and yellowed in others. There were odd stains on the floor that I didn't even want to guess the origins of. This was just the bathroom. One bathroom.

The rest of the clubhouse wasn't much better. Everything looked okay on the surface, but the minute you focused on anything too long, it became obvious that there were problems hiding under the surface, or even at surface level. It went a bit deeper than dirty couches and people fucking out in the open.

The brothers were nice enough. Some were rougher than others, and while they'd all been relatively good to me, there were only a few who would make decent father material. It was doubtful that the few that could be good would be the one to father my child. That was the biggest problem of all.

If there was a way to know for certain that it was Tripp's baby, I'd stick around. He may have only used me the once, but the soft spot I had for him had warmed even further into a full-blown crush on the man. Not that he'd noticed. He still pined over his long-gone wife. To hear the others tell it, Kim had been the love of his life. According to those same stories, she was a tough act for any woman to follow. As in, an impossible act to follow if you happened to be a club whore.

I closed my eyes and brought up the memory of my night with Tripp again. It wasn't the first time and most likely wouldn't be the last. Along with the memory came the wish in my heart that nine years without his wife had been enough to open his heart to someone else – even if that someone was a club whore.

Two months earlier

I GLANCED up through my lashes from across the room and tracked the club's president as he moved behind the bar to grab a bottle. Something was bothering him today and to anyone paying attention, it showed. To me, it definitely showed because I was always paying attention.

He started to head back to the hallway that would lead him back to his office, or maybe his bunk room as it was on the opposite end of the clubhouse to most of the others. When his gaze swept across the room, I lifted my head to make it known that I was not only watching him but waiting for him to take advantage of my services.

Tripp had never done so in the past, so there wasn't really a good chance he would take me up on the silent offer, but as his eyes locked with mine, hope grew in my chest. My heart ticked up a few beats per minute and before I could suffer another let down, Tripp crooked his finger at me.

I stood and my feet glided across the space between us as if being pulled by a magnetic force. When I made my way to within an inch of the man, he reached out and tugged me firmly to his side.

"You okay with this?" he asked.

"Of course," I insisted.

Tripp nodded before he quietly guided me back to his

room located at the end of a lonely hall full of offices and storage spaces.

"Last chance to back out," Tripp stated as we reached his bedroom door.

"Why on earth would I do that?"

He shrugged. "Never had you back here before." It was a mumbled line, but I heard it plain as day. What he really meant was that he'd never had me before. Not once. I would catch him watching me from time-to-time because my eyes would always drift to him if he was in a room. There was interest there between the two of us, but it seemed to be a fascination he was not inclined to act on until this moment.

Once the door was shut behind us, I turned and ran my hands up his arms and gently traced over his shoulders until my fingers managed to tunnel into his hair at the nape of his neck. Tripp's head tipped back as an inadvertent moan slipped free from his lips. "Feels really good, sweetheart."

"Why don't you make yourself comfortable and let me take care of you. You're always so tense with the weight of the club on your shoulders. Let me make it better for you tonight." What I really wanted to say was, 'Let me make it better for you forever.' That wasn't a sentiment that would fly with the club brothers though unless they were the one to claim you as their woman first.

"How are you planning on doing that, Vina?"

"I'm going to start out with giving you the best damn massage you ever had. We need to work out all this muscle tension and once your body is feeling good and loose, I'll help you work out your other frustrations any way you choose."

"Your first priority is taking care of me and making sure I'm not riddled with tension?"

"Yes."

"Is that something you do for all my brothers?" he asked while staring me in the eye and all but daring me to lie to him.

"No, it's not. You look like you need it though."

"It's not required."

My shoulders bounced as I offered up a smile. "It was just an offer. You're free to say, "No".

In answer, he started to pull his cut off and then lifted his shirt over his head and placed them both on what looked like an unused desk against the wall. His boots, jeans, and everything else were next. While he took care of himself, I stripped down to my bra and panties and then made my way to his ensuite.

"You have any lotion, oil, or lubricant in here?"

"Medicine cabinet."

There was a bottle of unopened massage oil with the seal still on it. He had at least been thinking about doing this with someone, at some point recently. I was happy to see the seal had never been cracked though. It would have sucked to know that I wasn't the only one who offered this up to him. It might not have been possible to tell him how I felt about the man who starred in most of my dreams, but I wanted to show him in some way that he mattered to me.

This little thing, giving him comfort, was the only way I had to do that. All the other girls would jump right into sex, thinking that was the only thing that made them worth the time the men spent with them. In most instances, that was probably true.

Tripp was laid face down on the bed when I returned with the oil. His face was cocked to the side, so he could see me when I walked back in the room. He smiled but otherwise didn't make a move. I sauntered over to the bed and then climbed on top and maneuvered myself so that my legs straddled his upper thighs.

"I'm going to start with your neck and shoulders because that is where your muscles look like they're nothing but hard knots." I trailed my fingers down his back gently, which caused an explosion of goosebumps to break out across his body. As I did, the other tense muscles also made themselves known.

"You have to take better care of yourself, Tripp. This is kind of ridiculous."

He grinned. "Not every day someone offers to give me a massage around here."

"Well, consider it an open invitation. If you need to relax, I don't mind helping you out." I wanted to add in any and every capacity but didn't want to sound like one of the desperate whores who were always trying to land a patch.

"I'll keep that in mind."

Before I poured the oil into my hands, I ran my fingertips over Tripp's scalp and gave his head a little massage. He groaned through it and more gooseflesh bloomed across his skin to let me know there were no pretenses in the noises he made.

As much as I would have loved to do that for him all night, there was more he needed from me. Despite the pleasure he took in those simple touches, his muscles were bunched into tight, hard balls of stress. I opened the massage oil and poured a generous amount into my hands and rubbed them together to warm the liquid before applying it to his skin.

I used my thumbs to kneed the muscles along his neck while my fingers dug in and vigorously worked the muscles of his shoulders and lower neck. "Fuck, that hurts so good," he muttered into the pillow.

"Shh," I whispered. "Just lie there and enjoy it. Relax. You're not the president in here. You're a man enjoying his night." That earned me another smile.

Over the next hour, I worked his entire neck, back, shoulders, arms, and even his ass and thighs before Tripp finally called the massage done. "Sweetheart, as much as I love your hands on me like that, because they're fuckin' magic, I think it's about time I showed my appreciation."

"I didn't do this for what I could get in return."

"Didn't say you did, Vina. Now come over here," he added ass he turned underneath me and crooked his finger again. "Get up here and let me show you how to relax, too."

I crawled forward awkwardly.

One thing I could say for most of the men in the club was that they were all about getting theirs and not a whole lot else. Maybe they were different with their old ladies when they took one, but with the club girls, the men rarely worried about whether we got off. Some of them would have us put on a show to get each other off, but I tried to steer clear of those situations because being with another woman wasn't something I enjoyed.

When I was hovering somewhere between Tripp's neck and chin, he reached up and grabbed my hips to pull me forward. It was only then that he realized I was still partially clothed, but he didn't bother to remedy that situation. Instead, he simply pulled my panties to the side and licked straight up my pussy lips before nibbling them at the top. He didn't attempt to part them and tease my clit yet. It's like the man wanted to taste me from the outside in.

I reached out and placed my palms on the wall behind the bed as he moved my body into the best position before he truly dove in and ate my pussy like it was his last meal and it was exactly what he ordered.

"Why does that feel so good?" I moaned the words, not expecting an answer, which was good because Tripp didn't give me one. Instead, he continued to lick, suck, and nibble my entire pussy from clit to taint and back again before dipping his tongue inside me and then starting over. Eventually, he latched onto my clit and sucked until zinging little electrical pulses shot from my sex and brought my muscles clamping down on the fingers Tripp had added to the action.

As the orgasm burned through me, Tripp flipped me over and pulled me down so that my head was the one resting on the pillow instead. He made quick work of getting my bra and panties off my body and then, before I could even blink, he was fully seated inside me and our eyes met.

"Perfection."

I couldn't have heard that right. Tripp just told me it felt like perfection to be inside me. The nerves I'd been stewing in the whole time I'd been with him suddenly dissipated as the butterflies inside my belly swarmed and went wild.

Maybe my infatuation with the man wasn't as one-sided as I'd always believed it to be.

His eyes stayed connected with mine as he thrust deep again only to slowly scrape his cock against my inner walls as he pulled back all the way to the tip. "Fuck, you feel so damn good, sweetheart."

I was speechless in my own little world of bliss as each thrust brought me closer to the edge again. "Tripp. God. So good," I mumbled into his shoulder as he began to pump harder. My arms wrapped around his upper body while I planted my feet firmly on the bed on either side of his legs to get leverage. Then, I managed to tilt my hips up to meet his thrusts that were coming more aggressively with each pump of his hips.

"Yes, baby. That's it, fuck me back," he demanded. I clutched onto his shoulders harder as we both pushed our bodies into attack mode. There wasn't a time in my past when I remembered fucking a man back so hard from the bottom. Just as the thought pinged around my brain, Tripp pulled out and flipped over so that he was on his back again and I was in the air before I realized what happened. He had me straddling his hips as he lined his cock up with my pussy and then yanked my hips down.

"Ahhh!" His cock sank deep in one solid thrust of his hips, and he pulled me down at the same time. Then, he stilled and waited until my eyes met his. The smile he gave me would have melted my panties right off had I still been wearing them.

"Ride me, sweetheart. Wanna see those tits sway as you bounce on my dick."

I followed directions well, though Tripp didn't watch my breasts bounce for him long before he reached up and started massaging the flesh and pulling at my nipples. With every pinch and tug the sensation felt as though it a line straight to the nerves in my pussy. My muscles clenched tight around Tripp's cock, and he hissed out a harsh breath.

"Fuck, baby, you keep doing that and I'm going to blow my load before you get off again."

"You keep doing what you're doing, and I'll get off again before you do." I promised him as my hips undulated harder as I angled just right to have him hit my most sensitive spot with each down-thrust I made. "I'm..." The words were lost on me as he tugged hard on both my nipples at once just as he thrust up and I came down hard on his cock. My head fell back as I shouted out my release and took Tripp over the edge with me.

As the euphoric feeling began to fade, I leaned forward and crashed against Tripp's chest. To my complete surprise, he didn't push me off or attempt to crawl out from underneath me. Instead, he rubbed his hands up and down my back and kissed the top of my head.

"You doing all right?" he asked.

"Mhm," I murmured. "Just basking in the afterglow. I can move." When my muscles flinched in preparation for me to remove my body from its perch on top of Tripp, he stopped tracing up and down my spine and held firmly to my hips.

"Don't want you to move. Stay like this, unless you're ready to leave."

"Not in any hurry to be anywhere else."

"Good." It was only then, after he stated that one word

with authority, that we finally moved. He pulled me down off his chest and to his side before he snuggled in behind me. When those strong arms of Tripp's wrapped around my body, it felt like heaven. Not only was a club girl getting off not a priority for most of the brothers, but there wasn't a single one of them who offered to cuddle me after sex. This was all new to me and for a brief moment, I wondered if this was the norm for Tripp. None of the other women talked about being with him, and to my knowledge, he had never taken one back to his room, but then again the way he pulled me in was done subtle and quiet-like.

Chances were, I would get the "keep this quiet" speech he must have given the others whenever he was done snuggling.

That was a cynical thought, but it was necessary to keep me from losing myself to a fantasy that only existed in my head. If only Tripp returned my longing to be with him.

As we laid there snuggled up with me as the little spoon to his big, he caressed my side and thighs in long, slow motions. "Do you dream about a life away from the club?"

"You kicking me out?" I teased.

"Nah, just wondering what kind of future you dream about, sweetheart. This life doesn't feel like a fit for you. Not as a club girl, anyway."

My heart ticked up a beat as hope pinged stupidly from the useless organ in my chest. My heart thought maybe he wanted me as his old lady, but my brain knew better.

"I had a shitty upbringing like most of the girls here. The club saved me when I needed saving and I'm here to do whatever I can to return the favor."

"You're not indebted to us, Vina. You know that right? You're free to go find whatever happiness you can at any time."

I nodded, but kept my face turned away from Tripp. No, there definitely wouldn't be ink and a patch in my future from him. He was all but pushing me out the door to go find someone outside the club.

"I'm a little confused. Do you not want me here?" I finally asked while trying to hide the hurt in my voice.

Tripp squeezed my hip and pulled me back into his body before wrapping me up in his arms again. "Nah, sweetheart. You always seem a little lost out there, like your head is anywhere but here. I wonder from time-to-time what you're thinking and if you wish you could be somewhere else."

"I'm perfectly content right here, right now," I told him. There was no way for him to know that I meant that in the most literal sense. It would remain my secret because Tripp wasn't like the other guys. He had an old lady once and knew how important it was to have a good woman at his side.

There was no way the club president would think having a club whore as his old lady would ever be a good idea, especially since I was only a few years older than his own kids. Maybe my age was why he was suddenly curious about my future plans.

I'd already tipped over the big three-oh and didn't miss the fact that most of the club girls were five to ten years younger than me. It made sense that people would start wondering about what my plans were. If we all blinked too long, I'd end up ringing in the big four-oh as a washed-up club girl as well. If nothing else came from this little tryst with the club president, it was the notion that I needed to start preparing for a different future because it was going to come for me sooner than later. And there was no way that the future I hoped for would come to pass, with me at the president's side.

It wasn't just about him being the president either. I was the furthest thing from a patch chaser you could get. Tripp did it for me. It was in his kind and thoughtful nature. He could be a vicious son of a bitch when crossed, but for those he cared about, he went the extra mile. I'd be a fool not to want someone like that who would respect our relationship, care for me, protect what's his, and do it all while looking dead sexy.

It was hard to shake those thoughts off as Tripp turned me to face him and leaned forward to nibble my bottom lip playfully.

"You were thinking too hard over there."

"Sorry."

He chuckled. "Don't apologize. If you don't want to share your future plans, you don't have to. It's not a requirement that you tell me all about how you're going to dominate in the world one day."

It was my turn to laugh. "You think a little too highly of me."

"If not taking over the world, what is your biggest goal?"

"Honestly?"

"Yeah, of course. No point in lying about what you want."

"I want a family."

"A family?" he questioned as his finger traced over my slightly furrowed brow. "That's it?"

"That's everything. I want a family who can count on me and who I can count on right back. I want to love and be loved and raise happy, healthy, well-adjusted children who will one day give me grandbabies to spoil." I shrugged my shoulders as if to brush off the serious wish with a bit of indifference. "That's been my dream since I was a little girl and it never changed."

"Well, hell, sweetheart, it doesn't take much to please you, does it?"

"I guess not, but to me it is everything. Maybe to someone else it doesn't sound like much," I argued in a much quieter voice.

"Aw, I didn't mean to offend you. Of course it's everything. Not enough people want to focus on family anymore. It's tough when most families need two incomes to make it. I was lucky that Kim was home with our kids most of their young lives until she was taken from us. They turned out pretty decent because their mom was always there for them. Don't think I'm making light of your dream. It was just shocking to hear."

"Because I'm a club girl?"

"Nah, just haven't heard someone share that dream in a really long time."

He didn't give me a chance to respond as his lips came down on mine. Something changed in the way he kissed me. It wasn't rough and needy like before. There was a gentler ease to the way he possessed my mouth, caressed my body, and then took me that second time. If I didn't know any better, I'd describe what Tripp and I did then as making love.

It was sensual, slow, and full of beautiful touches and sweet kisses.

Every time our eyes met, I would have sworn he was feeling the connection between us too. People couldn't just fake the intensity that brewed between us. Then again, when I woke the next morning, I was alone. There weren't any sweet notes telling me to wait for him to come back with breakfast and coffee. There weren't any texts or phone messages about needing to handle club business. He was simply gone, and I was left to go back to my life as a club whore. Only now, I'd had a taste of what being with a man who wasn't completely selfish felt like and it would be damn hard to go back to living the lie that I was happy as a club girl. The truth was, I was safe, and that lent to a certain feeling of contentment. I was far from happy though.

Thankfully, our conversation made me realize it was time to start saving for the future instead of squandering what I had.

I SNAPPED out of the memory with a pitiful sigh. If only I knew for sure that Tripp was the father of this baby. Unfortunately, there was the horrible possibility that the baby belonged to Tripp's son, Kip. What a mess. Despite knowing how it would hurt Scout, his ex-girlfriend, and another club girl, I would stick around if it was his, too. There were no romantic feelings about starting a relationship with the man. I knew his heart belonged to someone else and she was very much alive and in our faces. Still, he would make a good father, and we could raise our child as coparents easily enough.

I might have been tempted to stick around if there was a way to guarantee either one of the Martin men had fathered my baby. The sad truth was that it could be Bagger, Breakneck, or a few other members. None of them were ready to be parents. A few wouldn't step up even if the proof was shoved in their faces. I had to be around two months pregnant or so, if my periods-or lack of-was anything to go by.

It was the end of December. That put me possibly getting pregnant back in October. It was hard to say when exactly that happened, and I wish that I knew, because it would make all the difference in figuring out who the potential father might be.

The new year was three days away, and the club was holding their annual blowout party later, since the new year would fall on a weekday. That meant I had to get packed and get gone before anyone found out. They couldn't know because I couldn't have my child tied to the club forever when their father would probably never claim me. It would ruin my chances of finding someone who might one day love me.

I knew what I needed to do, and oddly enough, it was the club's own princess who inspired me. Her father – The Savage Viper's President – talked about her often enough, as did her uncle – SVMC's Vice President. They were proud as hell of Star Martin. She left this club, thwarted their efforts to keep a tail on her, and she ended up super successful all on her own. That was what I would have to do for my baby. I'd prove to myself, my child, and anyone else who cared that I could do it on my own. It wasn't like I was really breaking a rule. I didn't know who the father of my baby was, so there was no one to tell.

I just finished tossing all of my clothes and toiletries into my bags when someone knocked on my door. "Vina?"

Shit. It was Tripp, the club's president. He'd never been mean to me or anything, and we had only slept together that one time, but I worried what he would do when he realized I was going to bolt.

"Yeah?"

He opened the door and his eyes immediately traveled to my bags. "Well, I was going to ask if you were okay to handle brothers from our other chapters on New Year's, but it looks like you have other plans."

"I was going to come tell you." It was a lie and we both knew it.

"You don't owe anyone here any explanations, Vina. You're here because you want to be. When that time ends, it does. You're one of the good ones, so I'm guessing the brothers are going to be sad to see you go, but no one here will stop you."

"Thanks. Can we not make a big deal of it? I'd like to just leave quietly."

"Where are you going?"

I shrugged my shoulders. "I want to go to school and see if I can get a career for myself." I chuckled. "I'm thirty-years-old and not getting any younger. Besides, one day, I want to have a family of my own. Can't do that when I belong to everyone and no one all at once."

Tripp nodded his head. "Understandable. Are you sure you're good to go and able to get yourself started off?"

I wasn't, but he didn't need to know that. I'd figure things out. The club paid us a weekly stipend for helping out around the clubhouse. They couldn't and wouldn't pay us for sexual favors, but those of us who cooked or cleaned received a weekly salary. I wasn't a fool and took the chance to earn extra money just in case something ever happened. Still, I'd also stupidly spent a lot of what I made on clothes and other useless things. I had $2,000 saved and wasn't dumb enough to think that would last very long.

"Take this, and if you need help, don't hesitate to call me," Tripp said as he handed me a wad of cash. "The side door is your best bet to avoid a scene with your bags. We have a few members due back in about an hour, then it will start getting crowded, so..."

"I'll be gone in five minutes," I promised. The promise was to myself, but Tripp nodded his head and left my room without even glancing back. I didn't bother looking at the cash he'd put in my hand until he left. There was $2,500 in the wad he'd placed in my hand. Tripp didn't know it, but he'd just handed me a lifeline. It would cover a nice one-bedroom apartment until I could find a job to help cover the monthly expenses.

I glanced into the slightly warped mirror hanging on the back of the door to the bedroom I'd occupied for a little over a year. "Well, baby," I said to my still flat tummy, "it's just the two of us now. Don't worry, I'm going to take the best care of you. I promise."

I glanced back at the clubhouse one more time as I left in

my beat-up old Chevy pickup truck. It was another worry I'd have for some time in the near future, because the thing had been on its last leg for a while. Kip promised to have a look at it for me, but never got around to it, thanks to club business and heartbreak over his recent breakup with Scout keeping him busy.

"I wish Tripp was the one," I lamented again as I blew out a quick breath and then left the clubhouse for the last time. There was no use in looking back in the rear-view mirror. My past would stay right where it was, and no one would miss another club girl who disappeared on a whim. Not even the man I'd stupidly grown feelings for.

CHAPTER 5

DAVINA - 5 MONTHS LATER

"Kɪᴘ ᴋɴᴏᴄᴋᴇᴅ up that Ashlynn cunt while he and Scout were on a break, and all hell broke loose."

"Oh, no! Poor Scout. She must have been devastated. Where did she go?"

"What do you mean?" Dee asked.

"She couldn't stay there and see them playing happy family with the club," I suggested. To my horror, Dee shrugged her shoulders. I couldn't believe Scout could stick around to see that. No matter the problems she and Kip had, they were meant for one another. If I was honest with myself, it was one of the reasons why I walked away from the club so quickly. While Kip would have been one of the best options for a baby daddy, it would have destroyed my friend to know that I'd allowed him to have sex with me during their break, too.

"So, are you ever going to tell me who fathered your little miracle there?" Dee asked the question while pointing at my burgeoning belly. I was eight months along. My due date was

July 13th, which was only a few weeks away. I wasn't sure if the doctor was correct about that, because there were only two men I slept with during that timeframe. Tripp, during the one beautiful night we spent together, and Breakneck. I'd slept with plenty of guys a week or two later, especially around the time of the club's Halloween blowout, but according to the doctor, there was a little bit of wiggle room in the timeline. Still, I prayed my child didn't turn out to be Breakneck's mini me.

"It doesn't matter. This baby is all mine."

"You still don't know what it is?"

I shook my head. "No, the stubborn butt wasn't in the right position when I went for the ultrasound, and we couldn't see."

"Didn't they do another one?"

I shook my head again, feeling ashamed of my situation. "I, um, couldn't afford it."

"You know, if you told them that you're having a club kid, they would cough up the money for things like that until they could find out who the daddy is."

"Could you imagine if the dad was Breakneck or..."

"Say no more," Dee said as she cut me off. "You're right," she giggled, "heaven help that child if it belongs to that man. He's a lost cause."

"I know it's asking a lot, but please don't tell anyone, Dee."

"I would never," she sighed. "While I think the club would be able to help financially, I understand you not wanting to go through the bullshit of finding out who your little nugget belongs to and then having to deal with that person for the rest of your child's life." She shivered. "Honestly, it makes me want to double up on the birth control. I'd get my tubes tied if I didn't think I might want a family one day."

"Don't wait too long on that. The club will suck you dry if you let it," I warned.

"I know, sweetie. I'll get out from under it all, one day." She glanced down at her phone. "Crap, I really need to get back. I'll see you soon. Maybe by then, you'll know what you're having because that baby will already be here."

It was probable because there was no way I'd call or text to let Dee, or anyone else affiliated with the club, know when I gave birth. If I hadn't accidentally run into her at the mall on my trip to Augusta to get some last-minute baby things, then she wouldn't have even known I was pregnant.

Dee hugged me and left. I grabbed my things and waddled out to my car. The trip home would suck, because there was no way I could make it without having to stop and pee somewhere.

CHAPTER 6

DAVINA

"I'M EARLY. This can't be happening." To say I panicked when my water broke at work was an understatement. My boss, Mr. Avery, had to bring me to the hospital. Thankfully, he was a sweet, older gentleman who believed the father of my baby had abandoned us.

I hated lying to him, and assured myself it might not be a lie, depending on which club member fathered my child. Still, he took a chance on me while I was in school, and I didn't want to repay him by being untrustworthy. I interned with him, in a paid position, to be a paralegal. Once I graduated with my degree, I would get a nice bump in pay plus the ability to work from home sometimes. There was also the added bonus that Mr. Avery happened to practice family law, which might come in handy if anyone from the club ever found out about my baby.

"Your due date is July 13th. You're not that early. Everything will be fine," the nurse assured. "It's less than two weeks off."

"July 2nd. It's only July..." I had to stop arguing to breathe through another contraction. "July 2nd."

"Should I wait?" Mr. Avery asked. I shook my head. There was no telling how long labor would last, and I already knew the hospital would keep us for at least one night, if not two. Hopefully, there wouldn't be anything wrong with the baby because I didn't think I could afford an additional bill on top of what I already had to pay for my visits to the OB.

"Okay, I know your car is at the office, so give me a call when you need to get home, and I'll make sure Mrs. Avery gets the car seat installed."

"It's already installed in the back," I told him. "I just need someone to drive it to me when it's time to be discharged."

"We'll get it done."

"Keys are in my purse," I glanced down at the large bag beside me, and the nurse reached in to grab the keys. There was a single key to my car and one to the apartment that Mr. Avery and his wife also rented out to me. They had been a Godsend to me from the very beginning.

When I answered an ad in the paper about a small apartment space for rent in the same building where Mr. Avery's law practice was, I had to tell them that I was looking for a new job, too. When I mentioned that I was in school to get my paralegal degree, everything just fell into place. It almost restored my faith in humanity. Unfortunately, when you've lived the life I have, it's hard to turn everything around completely.

By the time Mr. Avery turned to practically run out of the hospital, I was wheeled straight back to a birthing suite.

By myself.

It was just me and the two lovely nurses who continually monitored my progress.

Just before they did a final check and told me I was ready to push, one of the nurses, Sarah, asked if there was anyone she could call for me.

"It's just me," I told her. That admission made me heave out great big sobs for how lonely I felt. It was the first time I wished to know for sure who the father of my baby was. It would have been nice to have the whole club here in the waiting room ready to welcome another member of their family. I wished Dee was in here with me. She was always my closest friend among the club women. I wished I had someone. Anyone.

The truth was, I hadn't had anyone truly in my corner since my mother died when I was fifteen. I never knew my father. The foster parents who were supposed to protect me failed and I ended up on the streets of Atlanta because of it.

I was on the streets for three years until I turned eighteen. Then, I moved up to living in squalor in apartments that shouldn't be available for humans or any other life form. Every time I tried to get ahead and get out of that situation, something would happen to keep me chained to the impoverished life. I was twenty-eight when the club took me in and had just turned thirty when I got pregnant.

I was about to turn thirty-one in two months, but not before my little one came along. At least I could say I beat teen pregnancy; despite the lifestyle I led early on while trying to survive. I didn't beat the odds at becoming a single mom, though.

"Okay, Davina, you can do this." Sarah coached me as she

used a tissue to wipe my face. "It's okay to cry in here, but I want you to know that you are amazing and you're being so brave. You have Neva and me in here and Doctor Harrington will be in shortly. We're all going to get you through this."

"Thank you," I whispered before another contraction hit. When it subsided, I grabbed her arm and pulled her close. "If something should happen to me, you need to contact the Savage Vipers MC. I'm not sure who the father is, but the baby belongs to the club. If anything happens, promise me you will let them know, so that I know the baby will be taken care of."

"You think a motorcycle club will take care of a baby?"

"Better than the foster care system ever will. I ran from that system after I was hurt, please, promise you won't let my baby go there."

"I promise to notify the club if anything happens, but there won't be any need. We're going to get you through this just fine."

A FEW HOURS LATER, I cradled my daughter in my arms while trying to get her to latch on to my breast.

"How are we doing in here?"

"Just fine. It was awful when they took her away," I admitted.

"Aw, sweetie, we would never let anything happen to your daughter."

While I wanted to believe the woman, I knew better. Portia was my new nurse. When they took my daughter to clean her up and do all the things they do to newborns, I'd been moved to a different room for recovery, which meant the labor and delivery nurses were no longer with me. Maybe it was naïve of me to think that I had bonded with Sarah during my labor experience. I was sure that happened to all new mothers, but still, for some odd reason, I expected her to travel with me to the other side of things.

"How is she doing?"

"I'm not sure." I tried to shrug my shoulders and Coral's mouth popped off my breast. She appeared to be sound asleep.

"You need to try to burp her, and then see if she'll try the other side. Always try to get her to take a little from each."

While I burped Coral and swapped her to my other breast, Portia looked over my chart. "As long as everything looks good tomorrow morning, Dr. Harrington will most likely release you both."

Her puckered expression let me know that she didn't like that idea. "Medicaid won't authorize another day unless there's an issue."

"I know." My sigh was heavy enough to disturb Coral. She pulled off my breast and started to whimper. "It's okay, sweet baby. Momma has you. Hush now, we've had a big day and it's time for you to rest up. You're going to need your strength for this life, so enjoy all the quiet moments while you can."

"Isn't that the truth?" Portia asked before smiling and heading back out into the hallway. "I'll be by in a couple hours. If you need me or feel too tired and want the baby to go to the nursery, just buzz us." She pointed to the call button that was positioned on the arm of the bed.

The nurse from the nursery tried to convince me to get rest and leave the baby with her earlier, but I demanded that my daughter be brought to me. I didn't trust them with her, and if that meant I got no sleep while I was in the hospital, then that was what would happen. I would sleep when my little angel slept after we got home.

CHAPTER 7
TRIPP

My gut twisted again, like it did the day I ran into June at the bank the first time. Maybe it was an ill omen, or perhaps just nerves over going out on a pseudo-date with my ex-girlfriend from high school. Again. Maybe it was because she was also a married woman. Maybe it was because of the last time we tried this. What happened after. The night I couldn't forget. The night that belonged to a different woman, one I hadn't seen in months.

"Fuck!" I breathed the word out quietly, thinking no one would overhear me until the sound of her chuckles reached my ears. I turned and grinned as she stood near the back of my pickup truck. I brought the truck, since my Harley was being worked on.

"Since you weren't even looking in my direction, I'm going to guess that was about nerves and not that I blew you away with my appearance," she teased.

I gave her a full-body once over and had to admit she looked great, though still a bit too prim, proper, and buttoned-up business class for my taste. "You look great. Just nerves, I guess. We've had our ups and downs, June.

She nodded thoughtfully. "Haven't you dated at all since..." The 'since your wife died' was left hanging in the air between us and again my gut clenched with the feeling like I was betraying my wife.

"No," I admitted. "Haven't been a saint in the years since, but never took anyone seriously." My gut clenched for a different reason then. There had been that one someone I wanted to take seriously, but it felt like there were too many obstacles in the way to make it work.

"I meant since the last time we tried this." She was fishing for information to see if I had been with anyone else.

"Not gone out on a date since then either," I stated. She could read between the lines, considering I hadn't said that I haven't been with anyone else. Not that it mattered. I hadn't been intimate with June since high school.

June pursed her lips and blinked away whatever thought creased her brows momentarily. As she took me in, her eyes lit up and down and my body with a fire she had no business possessing just yet. I was wearing my typical jeans, a t-shirt underneath a button-up, and my motorcycle boots. My cut was left behind, since I wasn't riding.

"I thought you might be on your motorcycle."

"It's in the shop right now," I told her. That much was true of one of my bikes, but not all of them. The same one that gave me the problems with shifting gears the day I met June was once again being a pain in the ass with a too stiff clutch and routine maintenance.

"You only have one?" she asked, and seemed as though she already knew the answer.

"No, I have more, but the truck seemed like the way to go." June, for whatever reason didn't seem happy about that.

"Oh, I thought we might go for a ride after..." She hinted at something that definitely wouldn't be happening.

"Only two women allowed on the back of my bike," I informed her. "My daughter and whoever I might take as my next old lady, if that ever happens again."

"I see," June stated with a bit of a pinched face.

"You're still married," I reminded her. "We're here to catch up, as old friends."

"We were more than friends once upon a time, and I apologized for the misunderstanding last time," she argued before pulling her temper back into check. Her whole demeanor made me wary of being there with her.

"Maybe this wasn't such a good idea. Sometimes, the past should stay buried. Our last attempt was likely a good warning."

She grinned at that, as if there was something amusing in what I'd said, before schooling her features and tipping her head to the side.

"I think the past has been buried for long enough. Let's go have a drink and if we get over the awkward stage eventually, maybe we can add dinner to the list, too."

I nodded my head and then pushed a hand out in front of me in invitation for her to head into the bistro restaurant after I reached to pull the door open. The little buzz of anxiousness gave me another jolt, telling me that this wasn't okay. I had to squash it, though. Even if June and I didn't end up doing anything more than this one outing where we got to catch up again, things were changing.

I was tired of being alone and lonely. Seeing my brother-in-law, Mack, and his wife, Viv, as they planned and prayed while she was going through her cancer treatments reminded me that life was short. It also reminded me what it was like to love someone that much and to have them return that feeling back to you. I missed it. I missed Kim, but she was no longer an option and I had to finally, really, let her go so I could grab onto a little happiness again. My mind strayed to Vina again too. I wondered where she was and if she found her happiness. That thought wasn't one I ever allowed to linger though. If it did, I'd have half a mind to chase her down and find out.

That was why I accepted this meet-up with June again. I couldn't get Vina off my mind. Fuck, it was probably a dumb idea, but I needed the distraction.

"I'm sorry if something I said messed us up tonight. It's honestly not as easy as I thought it would be to reconnect with you. The expectation is to fall back into a place where we were once upon a time-" I interrupted before she could finish her rose-colored glasses dip back into our history.

"Stop." I shook my head when June startled and attempted to ask me what was wrong now. "If we were truly starting from where we ended – and I'm talking about before anything happened between Kim and me – then we would be in a not-so-great place. It's one thing to think about the earlier times we were together, June. Yeah, at one point, what we had was fantastic, but it was also full of youthful folly and promises of the future that we were both too naïve to accept as not being realistic."

The waitress came up to our table and stopped me from barreling on into a topic that would probably end up upsetting us both and ending the night well before it started. Once she took our orders and left, I pulled June's hands into my own in the middle of the table. The shiver that ran up her arms was not reciprocated on my part, but I wouldn't ignore it either.

"It's obvious that you still have a strong attraction to me, but we aren't the same people we were back then. If you want to get to know the man I am today, then you need to put aside the boy you once dated. He doesn't exist anymore and hasn't for a very long time."

She nodded her head. "Trust me, I know. I'm not the same girl you knew either. Maybe it's harder to turn off the past for a woman."

"Don't give me that shit," I tossed out on a chuckle. "Men have feelings about things too, even if we don't share them openly or as often. Look, the girl I once knew was a beautiful part of my past. I'd prefer to get to know the woman she is today, though. If we can start from here, then maybe things will head in the direction you're hoping for. I refuse to look at us possibly hooking up again as a second chance. We took our chance back then and it ended when it needed to. This is an entirely different set of circumstances, not the least of which is the fact that you are still married – no matter how that came about or what you feel for the man.

"I'm not going to cuckhold some other dude. That's not a kink of mine, and if it's yours, then you need to find someone else. Most guys in the club would just take from you what you're offering and disregard the heart you wear on your sleeve. We can work on getting to know one another and being friends. If and when the time comes that you decide to end your marriage, we'll talk about what's next. When it's finished, we can become something more than friends, assuming things don't fizzle out before that happens."

"Tripp," she sighed. "I already told you my marriage isn't like that. In fact, Barry most likely won't make it home from his date with his mistress tonight."

"That is between you, Barry, and his mistress. What's between you and me is something entirely different. If you can live with that, then we can work on getting to know one another. If not, this will be the last time we meet."

"We can go at your pace." June tried to hide her sly grin behind her glass of wine the waitress put in front of her. Once she swallowed, she cast a sideways glance my way before chuckling lightly. "I think you might have forgotten how easily a divorce is obtained in Georgia."

"I've never known how easy it is to get a divorce in this state as I never thought about obtaining one."

That took her aback, and she dabbed her lips with a napkin in an attempt to hide her frown. "Sorry, I forgot that you embraced your marriage with the... With Kim."

I wasn't sure what she was about to call my late wife, but there was no way in hell I would tolerate anything less than respect.

"Sorry. Anna – you remember my cousin? Well, she and I have often referred to her as 'the homewrecker' over the years. It's inappropriate and childish. That should have never come out of my mouth, or even attempted to."

I allowed her apology to placate that anger that simmered just under the surface, and not for the first time tonight, I wondered what the hell I was doing here.

Then the thought of where I'd be, if not out with June, smacked me in the face. There was a part of me that tired of watching everyone else live their lives. The night spent with Davina back in October before she left was the last one I'd spent with a woman. There was plenty of pussy at the club, but it wasn't the same as having someone to come home to.

The night I'd spent with Davina had been half spent just talking about our days as we lie there together after some of the best sex I'd had in ages. Unfortunately, no one had heard from Vina. She never kept in touch. Even if she had, a relationship between us would never be an option for all the reasons that made me talk myself out of going there before. Nothing had changed. I'd walked away before starting something more with her for good reasons.

"The past needs to be kept in the past." I managed to say to June as she continued to sip her wine and wait on me. "I won't keep rehashing it. If that's a problem for you, then we can both walk away now."

"It won't be a problem, I promise."

I nodded and we finished our food. Instead of talking about Kim, my kids, the club, or June's husband, we spoke about the little things in between those giant obstacles.

Eventually, the night came to an end, and I took June back to get her car and before she leaned down to get inside, she stood on tip toes and tried to plant a kiss on my lips. Her efforts were thwarted with a quick turn of my head. Instead of the open-mouthed kiss she had been going for, June ended up with a mouthful of my stubble for her troubles.

"You are still married. I was serious about what I said earlier."

She blushed, from what was clearly embarrassment, and then climbed into her car and took off. There was a part of me that wondered if I'd even hear from her again. The nagging feeling in my gut made me believe that would probably be for the best anyway.

CHAPTER 8
DAVINA

"WHAT DOES THAT MEAN?" My voice shook as I smoothed my daughter's hair back from her forehead. It had grown so much already, even though it felt like I gave birth to her just yesterday.

"We're concerned about Coral's health and safety..."

"So am I. That's why I brought her in here to find out why this is happening," I explained. The look of disdain on Dr. Markham's face angered me and I couldn't even understand why. Something was happening that I just hadn't pieced together yet. There were two nurses in the room with us, instead of the one that was usually there.

My heart fluttered in my chest as the door to the exam room was opened and a woman in a sleek, but rumpled business suit stepped inside. As my attention was drawn to her, one of the nurses swooped in and grabbed Coral from my arms.

"Stop!" I yelled. "What are you doing?" I reached to pull

my daughter back into my arms when Dr. Markham grabbed me and pulled me forcibly to the opposite side of the room.

"Heather is going to take your daughter to another room," he muttered in my ear.

"No! Why are you taking my daughter?"

As soon as Heather left the room with my daughter the door opened again to reveal two police officers.

"What is going on?" I asked as tears flowed down my cheeks and my heart hammered a panicked beat against my ribs. "Where are you taking my daughter? What is happening right now?" I begged someone to give me answers as the female officer moved forward, grabbed my arm, and twisted it behind my back.

"You are under arrest for child abuse and endangerment of your daughter, Coral Rose Perrish. You have the right to remain silent. Anything you say can and will be used against you in a court of law. You have the right to have an attorney. If you cannot afford one, one will be appointed to you by the court."

"What are you arresting me for?" I asked again.

"Child abuse," was the simple answer, but I didn't understand.

"I don't understand. My daughter... Where are you taking her? I brought her here to get help and you're taking her away and arresting me? This doesn't make any sense."

"Dr. Markham contacted me about suspected abuse of your infant daughter." The woman in the business suit looked smug as she spoke down to me like I was garbage.

"Suspected abuse? I brought her here because she keeps getting bruises all over her tiny body for no reason. If I put them there why would I bring her in here to find out why it was happening?" I yelled at her.

She simply looked down at the tablet in her hands and typed something in. "Coral will be remanded to the foster care system for now. Don't worry, she'll actually be taken care of while she's there."

"Excuse me? What? You can't put her in foster care. I was in foster care, and they did awful things..."

"Maybe you should have gotten some therapy then, so you wouldn't do those *awful things* to your own daughter," the woman snidely remarked.

"Now, Sandra, that's not necessary," Dr. Markham corrected the woman. How was what he had done any better? I'd brought my daughter to him in the hopes of figuring out why her skin kept bruising for no apparent reason. I put her down to sleep at night and in the morning, she would have more bruises.

"Something is terribly wrong with my daughter and instead of helping her, you're having me arrested?"

The officers escorted me out of the office via a back door, no doubt to keep me from making a scene in the lobby. "I need a phone call. I need to call my lawyer," I demanded.

The male officer laughed, as if someone like me couldn't have a lawyer on retainer. He'd be right if I didn't work for one.

"You'll get the opportunity to do so once you're booked into the system."

IT TOOK twenty-four-hours to get me out of jail and back home, but my daughter still wasn't there with me. She was in an undisclosed foster home, where she would remain, until our court date.

"Okay, sweet girl, don't worry, we're going to get her back."

"But what's happening to her in the meantime? She was already so bruised. I don't even know how it keeps happening. What if she's placed in a home where they hurt her more? What if..." I couldn't bring myself to say it. I couldn't bring myself to think of the fact that my daughter could die or be killed and there was nothing I could do about it.

"I promise you, I'm working with the child advocate right now to make sure that she is doing well and getting the care she needs, instead of her medical concerns being ignored the way they have been. And when I'm done with everyone involved in this case, you and your daughter won't have to worry about anything again. I promise you that. They messed with the wrong family, dammit!" Mr. Avery was red-faced when he finished his tirade.

"Go calm yourself, honey. I'll sit with Davina while you get everything sorted and check in on Coral."

Gloria, Mr. Avery's wife, was a Godsend on a normal day and her angel wings were showing as she wrapped her arms around me and held me together. "I need her to be here in my arms. Why are they doing this to us?"

"That bastard saw Medicaid and assumed a whole lot about a poor, single mother bringing in an infant with bruises all over her body. He'll rue the day he made the mistaken assumption that you could ever hurt that precious baby of yours. My husband will see to it that he can't afford to practice in this state any longer.

Mr. Avery came back into the room a few hours later. I'd only just dozed off from exhaustion when I heard his muffled voice as he explained something to his wife. Her startled gasp is what finally pulled me to full consciousness.

"What's going on?" I asked in a sleep-roughened voice.

"I have some news," he stated ominously.

"What happened? Is she okay? Where is my baby?"

"She's in the hospital right now."

"Noooo!" I moaned. "What did they do to her?"

"Nothing, Davina. The woman fostering her was startled to see fresh bruises after Coral was put down for a nap, and she took her into the hospital and explained the situation. She went against protocol and contacted me directly because she wanted me to know that she didn't think you had anything to do with it and the doctors agreed with her. Dr. Jenkins happened to be doing rounds in the hospital."

At my blank look, Mr. Avery sighed. "Dr. Jenkins specializes in pediatric oncology."

"Oncology?" I asked.

"He handles pediatric cancer patients, Davina."

His voice was so soft when he relayed that information to me, but it sounded like someone just blared an alarm in my ears. "W-what..." It was all I could get out.

"He is running some tests, but they think that Coral

might have a form of cancer, a type of leukemia, and while it's rare for one so little to have it..."

Any further explanation was lost on me as I openly wept for my daughter whose life had already been such a struggle. She would never know her father because I also didn't know who it was. She would never have any family beyond me and the Averys who had sort of adopted us. And now, my precious baby girl was sick, and I stood accused of abusing her when I'd just been trying to get her the help she needed.

"Give her a minute," Gloria said as she came and wrapped me in her embrace once more.

"I need to see my baby. Please, tell me I can go see her now," I begged.

Mr. Avery nodded at me. "I'm working on that. Dr. Jenkins put in a call to Judge Reynolds and is attempting to explain the situation. The charges should be dropped soon. The doctor feels it is impeding your daughter's health to have been ripped away from a parent who obviously cares a great deal about the child's health."

"I should be by her side now. She must be so scared. What are they doing to her? They're supposed to have my permission to do anything. They're supposed to consult with me about her health, not a strange woman neither of us knows. Why is it okay for a stranger to make those decisions for my daughter, but I got arrested for trying to help my baby?"

I couldn't stop the sobs from wracking my body. Everything felt raw and I'd never felt so helpless in my whole life. It had sucked giving birth to my daughter all alone, but that was nothing compared to this. I'd just been told she might have cancer and I couldn't even be there to comfort her and make sure she knew she was loved every minute she drew breath on this earth.

"I need to be with my baby," I whined again.

"Oh, honey, we're working on it," Gloria cooed softly to me as she petted my hair and rocked us both back and forth, as I would have done with my own daughter if she hadn't been snatched away from me. Gloria's warm tears mixed with mine to soak our shirts. The Averys were grandparents to my daughter in every way that mattered. Having them by my side for this meant so much, but nothing could soothe me. Nothing short of being able to hold my daughter in my arms again.

CHAPTER 9
TRIPP

June and I had been talking and going on the occasional lunch date for the past few months. Nothing had progressed beyond a rekindled friendship because despite her lack of concern over the fact that she wore another man's wedding ring, it bothered me that she was still married. We had already been down this road once before the previous year. She proved then that there was more to the eye than the picture she kept painting for me.

That was my concern until about five minutes ago, when I saw the man June was married to walking out of a hotel in Augusta with a woman on his arms who wasn't June. In fact, the woman looked suspiciously like June's cousin, but since I hadn't seen her in years, I could have been wrong about that fact.

As soon as he tucked the woman into her car and sent her on the way, he glanced up and noticed me watching him. With what looked like a deep sigh, he squared his pudgy shoulders and ambled his way across the street to where I'd been standing.

"I know who you are," he insisted immediately. "And from the look on your face, you know exactly who I am. June must have told you we don't have a typical marriage. You can inform her of my affair, if you need to, but she won't care." He shrugged his shoulders with all the indifference that gesture implied.

"Why stay married?"

The man chuckled. "Stipulations of the contract. If we stay married until her father kicks off, things go smoothly with us splitting the inheritance and going our separate ways." He eyed me curiously though and once again, that little nudge in my gut told me that there was something more disturbing about the situation than I originally thought.

"When I married her, I thought the arrangement would be tolerable. She seemed like a stable, likable, well-adjusted woman with a good head on her shoulders. Truthfully, my expectations were to be equal partners in business and maybe even develop a healthy appreciation for one another."

"So, why didn't that happen?"

"You."

"Me?" I asked, slightly startled by his response. "You've been married for years."

"Fifteen, to be exact."

"So, how did I factor in that? I was still happily married to my wife and raising our kids when the two of you entered into this arrangement."

"Yes, well, you might have forgotten all about June until

recently, but you have always been her favorite obsession."
He shook his head and then offered me a grave look. "Be
careful getting involved with a woman who is that obsessed.
There's something not quite right with my wife."

"Says the man who just put her cousin into a car after a
stay in a hotel with her." It was a bluff on my end because I
hadn't been sure that's who he had been with until that
moment.

The man nodded. "Indeed, I did. June's cousin has
passion and grace that my wife will never possess. My
marriage is nearing its end, and when it is over, I can finally
go live my life happily with the woman I truly love."

It was my turn to warn him away. "Knowing that whole
family, I think you might be barking up the wrong tree there,
too."

He grinned widely at me. "Neither of those women are
my true love," he admitted. "One of them is business, the
other is to scratch an itch until I can get to the one who got
away." He looked thoughtful for a moment. "Though,
considering all I know about June and her obsession, maybe I
should rethink rekindling things with an old flame. Maybe
when it doesn't work out the first time, it's not meant to
work out ever. In your case, I'd heed that warning, but something tells me you're too stubborn to take good advice from a
man who might be in the know - whether you respect his
position at all or not."

"I respected you enough not to sleep with your wife
while she was still your wife."

"No need to sell yourself short on my account in that
department. Maybe, trying to fuck that icy prude will remind

you why she is an ex and help you to get her back out of your system again, so you can move on."

He didn't wait around for me to say anything, and there was no need for me to jump to June's defense either. The two of them had obviously attempted a real marriage at some point before giving up on one another. It made me wonder if June would be the same as she had been when we were younger. Her prudishness back then had been somewhat endearing because I'd thought she was just being bashful thanks to inexperience and her mother's warped views of intimacy being pushed at her for so long.

Her husband's assessment made me question my judgement in considering the option of going there again. Then, Davina's pretty face popped into my thoughts. I couldn't have the woman I truly wanted because she was just too far out of reach, especially ever since she left the clubhouse. If attempting to move on with my ex managed to work thoughts of her out of my system, so it was easier to get over the 'what could have been' thoughts, then that was what I'd do.

Maybe, if I was lucky, things would be different, and we'd be able to make something of this second – I guess maybe third – chance we'd been given. That didn't stop me from feeling a little bit sick when I thought about introducing June to the kids, or for that matter bringing her around my VP - a man I still considered my brother-in-law. There was no way Mack would ever accept June back in my life. Still, something told me that I needed to keep her close for some reason that I couldn't put my finger on just yet.

Maybe it was fate sending me a message. My gut

instincts were screaming two very different things at me. Keep her close and send her packing. I wasn't sure which to listen to, and assumed most of the latter was due to our history and residual guilt I felt when I thought of my late wife. Time would tell which instinct I should have listened to. With both of my kids being back in town and our family finally together again, I didn't know how to navigate all the aspects of my life without rocking the boat, let alone sinking it.

CHAPTER 10

DAVINA

I was able to see my daughter for the first time since she'd been taken away from me, nearly a week later. Dr. Markham doubled down, along with the social worker, who were both insistent that it wasn't cancer my daughter was dealing with, and instead was abuse.

Even when the woman who fostered my daughter stepped forward and explained the new bruises on my daughter, they tried to say that they just hadn't bloomed before she was taken from me. It didn't help that the oncologist who diagnosed my daughter with a form of leukemia, that would be extremely unlikely and rare in an infant as young as her, had to go out of town on a family emergency of his own during this whole process.

The judge would not admit his findings without having him there to quantify them for the court in person. It was a ridiculous circus of events that kept me from my daughter and delayed any possible treatment for her.

Mr. Avery swore up and down in court that we would sue

Dr. Markham, his staff, the social service worker, and anyone else who kept me from my daughter and stood in the way of getting her the treatment she needed. When Coral's foster mother tried to go against them, and take Coral to a different hospital, my daughter was removed from her care as well.

The one thing I didn't do, that may have sped the process along, was to go to the media as Mr. Avery suggested. There was no way in hell I wanted to do that and put my face out there along with the plight of my child, and abuse allegations, when all it would take was one member of the club, or someone affiliated with them, to connect the dots and a whole new shitstorm would fall upon us.

If I thought it was hard to get my daughter back in my care, and to get her the medical attention she desperately needed, then it would become unfathomably harder if we added a motorcycle club, and innumerable possible baby daddies to the mix.

Finally, Dr. Jenkins made it back to town and when he went to check on my daughter and realized she was no longer on his ward, he started making inquiries that landed us back in court, where finally - FINALLY - the judge listened and got the ball rolling on dismissing the charges against me and allowing my daughter to be treated for the cancer she had, rather than just being watched while the signs of her supposed abuse failed to fade.

It took far too long before I was able to hold my baby again, and even then, it was a bittersweet moment because I wasn't actually able to hold her tight and love on her the way I wanted due to fear that I might inadvertently harm her.

She looked so fragile. My baby girl, who aside from a few

unexplained bruises a week ago, had been healthy when I last saw her was now thinner looking. She didn't seem as vivacious as usual.

"Oh, my sweet baby girl, I'm so sorry Momma wasn't here for you for these past couple weeks. I promise to never let you go away from me again, no matter what I have to do to make that a reality."

A throat cleared behind me and I turned to see Dr. Jenkins enter the room. "Miss Perrish, I'm terribly sorry that everything happened the way it did. If I had known..." He looked away, almost guiltily. "Well, I can't say I still wouldn't have gone, as my family was in crisis, but I would have made sure one of my colleagues was more aware of the nuances of the situation. It never occurred to me that Dr. Markham would challenge my findings while I was away. You have my most sincere apologies."

"The only person who owes me an apology is Dr. Markham. Well, his staff and social services do as well. I just don't understand how they could have prolonged this when another doctor diagnosed my daughter with..." I couldn't bring myself to say it.

"Acute Myeloid Leukemia." Dr. Jenkins sighed as he filled in the words for me. "I can almost understand Dr. Markham's hesitation, since it doesn't generally appear in one as young as your daughter, but we all know that there are no absolutes in medicine - or at least we should. It was obvious that you were concerned for your daughter, so I'm not sure why he was so adamant that it was a case of abuse - even to go so far as to say I had misdiagnosed your child." He shook his head.

"Truthfully, I'm not even supposed to speak to you about him, since your lawyer already started legal proceedings and the hospital is culpable in them as well." He shrugged his shoulders. "It's clear," he stated while staring down at my daughter, "that the week's delay took a notable toll on Coral, though. So, I don't give a damn what they have to say about me bad mouthing a doctor who caused that delay in treatment with his asinine assertions."

I offered a weak smile to the man as he went about checking my daughter over. "I know you were reluctant to give the information to social services, but we really could use the father's information. Either his, yours, or potential siblings' DNA could be the key to making your daughter better."

"Can I be frank with you, without ending up in cuffs?"

He grinned, as if I was joking, though I wasn't.

"I promise, anything you have to say that will help your daughter, is nothing I will judge you for. Definitely won't be anything I'd call the law for either."

"How can you be so certain?"

"I'm a fantastic judge of character, Davina. You've done nothing but fight *for* your daughter. That's all I want to do here. Give her a fighting chance."

I nodded my head and explained my situation. To my surprise, he didn't judge me at all. Instead, he pulled a stool over, took my hands in his, and talked to me like I was on his level instead of on the lowest rung of the socio-economic ladder while he was miles higher.

"We can have the lab set up to take as many DNA samples as necessary to test for paternity. Actually, we can let them know we'll be testing potential bone marrow donors and to expect and influx of bikers soon." He winked at me. "No one else in the hospital has to know that we're searching for the father. Those men don't need to know either, if you can convince them to show as potential marrow donors." He sighed then and squeezed my hand. "The father will find out when the results are done, as we will have to ask him a few questions to see if we can get closer to a good match."

"So, she really does need a bone marrow transplant?"

"Most likely."

"Why can't I do that?"

"We will test you, but parents are rarely a good match. You usually only carry half the markers we're looking for, and while it may be good enough to attempt in a dire situation, we want to find a closer match, if possible."

"A sibling?"

"If there is a full-blood sibling, they're usually the best chance."

I shook my head once more. "That's not possible. She's my only child."

"Is there a possible half-sibling? They might not be a perfect match but could possibly have more markers than a parent would."

"It depends on who the dad is," I stated as my cheeks heated with embarrassment again.

"Davina," he offered calmly. "Don't be embarrassed on my account. You lived your life the way you wanted to, and from all accounts, you did so in the safest way possible. Things happen even when we're being careful. Don't beat yourself up over why there are possibilities. There are people who simply don't have a clue where to start, and we work with what we have. No judgements, I promise. I know that's a hard thing to believe after what you went through this past week, but it's true."

He patted my leg and stood. "I'm going to give you time with your daughter." He glanced at the clock. "She'll probably be up to eating within the hour. Let's see if she does better with her mom here to offer her a bottle. I have a feeling some of her failure to eat and thrive was due to missing her mom"

"I was breastfeeding her," I stated sadly. "They had no right to stop that."

His warm hand landed reassuringly on my shoulder where he gave a little squeeze. "I have no doubt that your lawyer will make them pay dearly for that. Remind him to add this as another problem the delay in getting you to your daughter caused, especially if no one even bothered to ask you to pump breastmilk for your daughter while she was outside of your care. Your inability to breastfeed your daughter set her health back further than if you'd been able to continue. I will testify to that fact, if need be."

"I will let him know. Thank you, Dr. Jenkins, for everything."

"Anything I can do to help, you just let me know."

He left after that, and I immediately texted the information to the Averys so that they would know, and I wouldn't forget.

Hours later, I couldn't delay my own needs any longer. My stomach growled relentlessly and made me feel a bit queasy. I got up and went to the cafeteria where I ran into a woman who eyed me speculatively at first. Then, she seemed more determined as she threw her shoulders back and came toward me.

"Didn't you used to hang around the Savage Vipers clubhouse?"

"Why?"

"Sorry, Bagger and I are together."

"How could you possibly know I was associated with them?"

"I thought you looked familiar. I've seen your picture or something," she insisted. That was weird, but truthfully, she looked like one of the rich girls who used to come to open-house club parties as a 'fuck you' to their parents' rules or whatever.

"What can I do for you?"

"Are you sick?"

"No, my daughter is."

"Does she belong to a member?"

I glared at the woman for a moment and then decided, 'What the hell?'. I had nothing to lose anymore because I'd set my pride aside, give every ounce of my blood, money, and anything else I could gather to keep my daughter alive. I told her my story, starting with my finding out I was pregnant and leaving before I had to figure out who the father was, and ending with how that information was now desperately needed to save my daughter's life.

"I bet it was Bagger. He sometimes forgets to wrap it up," she muttered under her breath, as if I wasn't supposed to hear her. For some reason, I doubted her. When our eyes met, she must have seen the wary look on my face. "Sorry, I didn't mean anything by it. We had a pregnancy scare at one point, that's why I said that."

I still didn't know if I could believe her, but she popped up and offered her hand. "I can take you to Bagger's place. It could be a good starting point for you, so that you don't have to drag all the men through DNA testing, if it isn't necessary. He would go in and get it done without question. Probably in the hopes of checking himself off the daddy list, but he also has a big heart. If he is the daddy, he will do everything in his power to make sure she survives."

"Why are you helping me? Didn't you say you're his girlfriend?"

"Yes, and while it would suck to know he had a baby with another woman, what would it say about me if I knew there was a possibility and didn't tell him. I mean, he might think I'm disloyal for trying to help hide a club baby." I flinched at that because soon enough my daughter's father – whoever he turned out to be – would be wondering the same thing about me.

The woman continued on despite my thoughts. "Plus, if there has to be a stepmom in the picture, you want me to be that woman. I won't try to claim your child, or get in your way, but I will be there as a support system for you both."

Her smile seemed genuine. I glanced down at what was left of my food and grimaced. I'd eaten enough to fend off the waves of dizziness but couldn't stomach anything further.

"Okay. I can go with you to Bagger's. I need to figure this out for my daughter's sake, and I need to go home and get a shower and fresh clothes, too."

"Perfect. Let's go, so you can get back to your daughter sooner and I can find out if my man is her daddy or not. I know I seem cool with this situation, and I promise not to give you any trouble, but I'll feel better once we know for sure."

I could understand that.

By the time we arrived at Bagger's house, the woman, who told me her name was Missy, seemed far more nervous than I was. So much so that when I went to get out of the car, she didn't budge.

"Are you coming?"

She shook her head. "I'm going to stay here until one of you comes to get me. I think this is something you need to confront him with alone, so that he is more apt to tell the truth about being a possible father. If he gives you a hard time, I can come be there, obviously."

"You're far more trusting of your man than I think I would be in this situation."

Missy smiled at me. "Well, you seem to be going through enough right now. Even if he did try something with you, that would be a problem between he and I."

I nodded and got out of the car. It felt like a brick had settled into my stomach. A lead brick that maybe had little chunky brick babies to weigh me down too. The walk to his door felt like I was headed to the gas chamber after eating my last meal. I did not want to do this.

I knocked on the door, but no one answered. I was about to turn and walk away but could have sworn I heard something or someone thump around inside. I banged on the door harder, thinking maybe they just didn't hear me the first time.

"What the fuck?" A woman called out as the door was slung open wide as possible. I knew exactly who she was on site, even though we hadn't met before. Tripp's daughter was standing there in the doorway, dripping wet, obviously fresh from a shower at Bagger's house, while his sweet girl-friend, Missy, was waiting in the car for me to talk to her man about the fact that he might have a daughter with me. What was Missy going to think? She wasn't worried about him cheating on her with me, but he had another woman in his house, and she was obviously comfortable being there.

"Can I help you?" Star asked, and there was nothing polite about the way she did so.

"Who exactly are you?" I asked. Not that I didn't know who Star Martin was, but honestly, I wanted to know what the fuck she was doing showering at Missy's old man's house.

"Hang on, I'm praying for the Lord to give me strength, right now," Star huffed sarcastically. If she wasn't the other woman that I would have to tell Missy about, her attitude might have made me smile.

Instead, I was pissed that I would have to break the heart of the sweet woman who brought me here to try to help me and my daughter, even if it might make her life messy. "Where is Bagger? I need to talk to him now!" Yep, I might have been a club whore, but I hated cheaters in any other setting. Truthfully, I hated myself on the rare occasion that I had to lay down with a club brother who I knew to be involved with someone. The fact that the president's daughter would willingly be the other woman kind of threw me into bitch mode. She had the opportunities to make better choices that I had not been given.

"I'll go get him and be right back." Start turned and shut the door in my face at that point. I stood there with my arms crossed over my chest to wait. What else could I do?

"Get your inner judgy bitch under control, Vina. You're not helping yourself by pissing people off." I whispered the words to myself in the hopes that my own warning would sink in. It wasn't my place to judge what a club brother had on the side or who they had on the side. It didn't really matter, so long as I could get someone to donate bone marrow to keep my baby girl alive. "She is the goal." Another reminder.

"Can I at least come in to wait? It's about to rain out here," I yelled through the door.

"No!" Star yelled back before she called out to one of my potential baby daddies.

"Jared!" I could hear the exasperation in her voice even through the door. "There's some woman here to see you."

"Where?" I heard him ask.

"Outside, where she belonged. I don't know her, so she didn't get an invite in."

"Your house, your rules." Jared told her. I glanced back at Missy's car with a worried look on my face. That didn't sound much like he considered Star to be a side piece. It sounded like she might be living with him.

"It's your house" the woman countered.

"Nope. It's our house, and when it comes to other women knocking on the door, it becomes your house. You make the rules. You don't want someone inside, they don't come in. Period."

"You have become a very wise man."

"Yeah? Let me get dressed and see what this chick wants, then we'll work on all the other things I have to show you that can make you proud of me."

Seriously? Her house? My stomach twisted again as more of those lead bricks settled into it. I glanced back at Missy's car once more. She was still sitting there. How could she be sitting there so calmly? She had to have seen that a woman opened the door. If she'd been around the club at all while dating Bagger, then she would even know who the woman was. Maybe. Star had been gone a long time. I didn't even know she was back in town until she opened the door.

"Do you want her inside?" I heard Bagger ask.

"It's about to rain, so there's no need for you to stand outside, but I'm not going anywhere if she comes in. If you're prepared for me to hear whatever she has to say, then invite her in. If not..." Star didn't give him what would happen "if not". It was obvious. Either he left me out in the rain to talk, ignored me completely, or allowed me in and we had to talk with Star present. Star. The woman who was the sister and daughter of two of my potential baby daddies. Shit was about to get messy.

"If not, we'll have a problem anyway. Twinkles, if a man came to the door wanting to see you, and you didn't want me to hear what it was about, I'd have an issue with that."

"Good to know we're on the same page then."

It really did not sound like Star Martin was the side chick

in Bagger's world. I glanced back nervously at the car Missy brought me here in just as the door to the house opened.

"Vina? What are you doing here?"

"Can I come in? Your whore of the day left me out here to get rained on." Okay, as the words snapped free from my mouth, I knew I should have clawed them back.

"First of all, you're going to drop the attitude about my old lady. Secondly, we never had anything between us, so no matter who I have in my house, it's not your fucking business to comment about them. We clear?"

"Yeah, sorry," I mumbled the apology as he stepped aside to let me in. I glanced around and then brought my eyes back to Bagger, avoiding Star altogether. "Looks different since Breakneck moved out.

"You been here with Break?" Jared asked.

"Twice," I confirmed.

"Well, he doesn't live here anymore, so I'm not sure why you thought it was okay to stop by my house."

I had to remind myself that I was doing this for my baby girl. I fidgeted with a lock of my hair as I tried to find the right way to approach this, especially since he'd just called Star his old lady. Maybe Missy was the other woman and Star didn't know. Was I supposed to tell her? Fuck. It felt like no matter what I did or said at this point that these people would never be inclined to help me or Coral.

"I wouldn't have ever bothered to find out, but things have changed, so..."

"What are you talking about?" Star huffed, obviously frustrated with my presence. I couldn't say that I blamed her at this point. Apparently, I'd been brought to this house under false pretenses, even though I had a very real, pressing matter to discuss.

"I don't know her. Can she go to another room or something? This is personal." It was the truth. I didn't know Star, and honestly, I didn't' want her flipping out on me when I told Bagger that Missy was the one who brought me here. My baby was sick in the hospital, and I didn't need to be hemmed up on charges if Tripp's daughter decided to fight the messenger.

"If you think something personal involves me, then she's going to know about it whether you say it in front of her or five minutes after you leave, so just get on with it."

"Bagger," I pleaded, knowing how messy it was going to get. "Please, I don't want your whore in my business."

"What the fuck did I just say to you at the door?"

I flinched back from the venom in his voice. "Sorry, it's just, this has nothing to do with her."

"Vina, shit or get off the pot! You got something to say, spit it out now because my patience is wearing thin."

"I have a daughter."

"Okay, and?"

"She's in daycare right now, that's why she isn't with me." That last line was a lie, but I didn't want to drop the cancer bomb on him before I got him to agree to a DNA test. I wasn't stupid. A sick kid would send some men running quicker than any other potential kid.

"She's trying to tell you that you're her baby daddy," Star offered with a little less attitude.

Jared's head turned so fast to look at Star, that I almost couldn't track the movement. "What the fuck?" He then turned back to me and if looks could kill, my poor baby would be an orphan.

"See, this is why I didn't want her in here. It's not her business and I was trying to break the news gently."

"The only person I've ever stuck my bare dick in is standing right behind me." Jared jutted a thumb over his shoulder. I shook my head at that.

"No, I think there was once," I attempted to say.

"Never!" he argued without hesitation. "I've never fucked you, or any other club girl, bare. You know better." He paused, as if in thought and then carried right on with his explanation. "I only remember being with you once about a year or so before I got with Missy. Halloween party before..." His words trailed off and I nodded my head.

"Yeah, that's why I came to see you. My daughter was born on July second last year."

"I wasn't the only man you were fucking back then. You were a club girl, living on site, any of my brothers could be your baby daddy, or hell, someone else entirely. I don't know what you got up to when you weren't at the club. If you think I'm just going to accept the fact that you seem to want to pin this kid on me, you are dead fucking wrong."

"I'm certain that it was you," I told him. "Missy even said that my daughter looked like you when she saw us in the store the other day." I winced at the outright lie I just told. Missy had hinted at that, but it was in the hospital today. I was probably going to hell, but if my daughter got the chance to live, then I'd deal with the eternal flames.

"Missy?"

I nodded. "She drove me here. I couldn't remember

where the place was because Breakneck brought me before. I never paid attention."

"Missy brought you here?"

"Yeah, she's outside in the car." I pointed back to the door in explanation.

Jared turned and all but ran for the door. I wasn't sure what he was going to say to Missy but didn't really have a chance to follow him and find out either because Star moved to stop me. "I wasn't around when you worked at the club house, but I used to live there. Tripp is my dad."

"If she brought you here, she's long gone now," Bagger said as he came back into the house.

"There was a silver Mercedes parked outside when I answered the door." Star informed him.

"Son of a bitch," he growled.

"Vina?" Star called out my name as if it was a question.

"It's Davina. Davina Perrish."

"Davina, I know that woman probably put shit in your head, and made you a bunch of promises, but the likelihood of Jared being the father is slim, you have to know that."

"It's still a possibility and I need to know now."

"Why? Why do you need to know now?"

I guess there was no getting around it. "She has cancer." A wave of sheer sadness and terror swept over me and there was no way I could hold it all in anymore. The lead bricks in my stomach were too much to bear on top of this whole shitty situation. That bitch sent me here to cause havoc for a club brother. Her ex-boyfriend, according to Bagger. Shit. Shit. Shit. At this rate, no one from the club would help me or my daughter.

"That's some more shit that Missy probably fed her!"

"No," I cried out to Bagger.

"What can we do to help?"

I shrugged my shoulders and watched through teary eyes as Jared paced across the room from us. Star came over and put her arm around me and pulled me into her body in a comforting gesture.

"Obviously, a DNA test has to happen. Considering you worked for the club, we will go over there and ask the men that you slept with around the last two weeks of October and first two weeks of November to take a test. We can't force them to, but it's the best I can offer you."

I cried into Star's shoulder even harder. "W-w-why would you help me?"

"Sweetheart?" she waited until our eyes met to continue. "Were you with my dad or brother around that time?" I nodded, slightly embarrassed that I had to admit to that while crying in this woman's arms. "Okay, so that means three of the men in my life could possibly have fathered your child. If it's Jared, that might be my stepdaughter one day. If it's Kip or Tripp, it could be my niece or my sister. If you're looking for the father, I'm assuming you're looking for a match for a donation?"

"Bone marrow." My answer was almost whisper quiet because it felt like admitting that made it more real than our situation already was.

"Okay, well, I will go in and get tested right away. You tell me when and where. If I'm a match, I'll gladly donate."

"Why are you being so nice?" I sniffled and hated that I

sounded so whiny. I just had no more energy to fake being okay.

"Honey, if I'm a match, she's most likely my kin."

"Sorry, Vina. Missy's been causing problems lately. I shouldn't have taken it out on you. We'll get the tests done. If she's my daughter, you know I'll take care of her, and see if I'm a match. I have to ask that you don't try to bring her around until we know something though." Bagger was nicer to me now that he knew his ex must have painted a different picture for me before dropping me off on his doorstep.

"I understand. I don't want her to know until it's confirmed anyway."

Jared nodded. "You know that you're going to have to answer to the club for keeping her a secret, right?"

"I know." I stared down at the ground, unable to meet either of their eyes. Technically, the club could take my baby from me and if they saw fit, eliminate me altogether for the breach of trust. Coral was undoubtedly a club kid. Most of the men treasured their children when they had them and the rest of the club doted on them.

"Let's get you a ride home since the one that brought you here took off." Jared told me. "Word of advice, stay far the fuck away from Missy. She's interfered one too many times now, and things aren't going to go very well for her from here on out."

"Okay, thanks. I'm sorry about her. I really didn't know. She made it sound like you were still together and that she was giving me a chance to talk to you alone." I turned my attention to Star then. "That's why I had attitude with you when you opened the door. It's one thing for the guys to be with the club girls, but to openly cheat on their women..." I let that hang in the air.

"Honey, there is not a difference to me. If this idiot gets caught with a club girl here, on the road, or wherever he won't be my man anymore."

I smiled at her boldness. It was nice to know she was strong and secure enough in who she was to take that stance. "I wish I had been like that. Might have saved me some heartache along the way."

CHAPTER 11
TRIPP

"I want you so bad right now," June admitted to me.

"The feeling is mutual, but we can't."

"Oh, we most definitely can," she insisted as the infuriating woman tugged at my belt buckle. I stopped her with my hands over hers and eventually managed to bring hers up between our two bodies near my lower chest, away from my suspiciously absent erection. It was weird that my body didn't respond to her, but that could be because I have these thoughts in the back of my head about how I don't want to be the other man in her life.

"We can't because things need to be settled with your husband before we go there."

June threw her head back as she laughed boisterously as if I'd just told her the world's funniest joke. "I'm being serious."

Her laughter tapered off as she took in the tone of my voice and the fact that I was indeed serious. "You're kidding, right?"

"No," I shook my head. "I mean it. I don't want to start us off with an affair or a scandal."

She scoffed at that. "Isn't that how you started things off with your ex-wife?"

"My deceased wife, not my ex. And did it occur to you that I learned a lesson from how things started with Kim and me."

"Don't say her name," she demanded in a humiliated whisper.

"She was my wife. I have kids with her whose lives I am very much involved in. If you can't stand to hear her name, then this will never work between us anyway."

I could see June's attempt to pull in her temper. "It's still hard for me to remember those days."

"Why?" It didn't really matter what her answer might have been. "Listen, June, either we're putting our past behind us and starting fresh here, or..." I left the rest hanging for her to fill in. It would never work to rekindle something if she was going to hold my teenage choices against me.

"If that's the case, then why are you so worried about my husband? He told me he spoke to you and told you that it was okay for us to be intimate."

I blew out a frustrated breath. "June, for exactly that reason. You are presently tied to him, and I shouldn't need another man's permission to go there with you. I don't want to be the other man in your present scenario. When we take things to the next level, I need to be the only man in your life. I told you, I learned my lessons where infidelity is concerned and there won't be a repeat performance, no matter which end of the chain I'm on."

She huffed and then sighed before her shoulders finally released all the tension they were holding. "It should make me happy that you feel that way, especially considering what happened to break us up."

"We were young. What happened with Kim only happened because we were already having problems back then. It was a symptom of our bigger issues, and we were too young to deal with them. I'm not that kid anymore, June. When something isn't sitting right, I'm of a mind that it needs to be fixed not shoved into the background."

She nodded her head. "I agree. I guess, I just thought that since he has his affairs, and we were married for convenience only, that it wasn't the same. I see your point, though. You're right. You deserve to start this relationship with a clean slate. No more history getting in the way and no other men. We already started the process. It doesn't take long in Georgia when the divorce is uncontested, but there are things we will have to work through. My inheritance and what he thought he'd be getting out of it is a big deal. I don't just want to see my father's bank go to my husband in a divorce. That wouldn't be fair to me."

"I understand that things are complicated. I'm not going anywhere, June."

Her hands shook as they reached for my own and held them tightly, pulling the two of us closer together again. "That is my biggest fear."

"What is?"

"That you will go somewhere else. That you'll get tired of waiting like..." She bit off the rest of it, clearly having been about to say something about the time she went to Europe, and how I didn't wait for her. Staring down into June's eyes, the worry hit me again that maybe exes should stay exes.

Nostalgia for an old flame was one thing, but to constantly be crucified for something I did when I was barely a man wasn't something I'd sign up for.

"I know what you're thinking," June whispered to me as her eyes came up to meet mine. "I promise, it's not that I'm holding it against you. There's just always this little bit of worry in the back of my mind. You know that little voice of doubt that tells me that I'm not good enough, or that I'm not worth the wait." She waved away my denial before I could even get it out. "I know. It's just in my head. You were right. We weren't in the best place when I left that summer. Even if everything else hadn't happened, there was no guarantee that we would have stayed together.

I would have gone off to college, and I know now that you would have never followed. Your club meant too much for you to leave it. That was something that I couldn't comprehend back then. They were your family, your livelihood, and I was just a high school girl."

"You weren't just any high school girl, June. You were my first girlfriend."

There was a glimmer of something in her eyes that looked a lot like triumph at my admission. It wasn't like that was ever a secret, though. We dated through most of high school, and I wasn't stingy with my feelings the way some of the club's brothers were at the time. Those crusty bastards seemed almost afraid to make a declaration of love to a woman. I didn't have that problem. By high school, there was no denying that life was short, and you had to tell people how you felt about them before you lost your chance. That much I knew, and I've lived by that.

A brief flash of the one time I didn't hit me square in the chest. I'd lost my chance to see if anything could come from a possibility with Davina. She shouldn't even come to mind while standing there with June. Still, it was one of the few regrets I harbored and one of the only times I kept my mouth shut about my interest in someone. There just seemed to be too many obstacles in the way at the time. Her age. The fact that she was a club girl. My kids and what they might have thought about it.

I shrugged the thought off and pulled June into my arms, as if to apologize for thinking of another woman yet again when we were trying to work through whether we should give it a try again.

"I really think this is finally our time," June mumbled into my shirt before placing a kiss over the President patch on my cut.

"Yeah? Even if we have to wait for your divorce to be finalized before we take the next step?"

"The way I see it, we'll have time to get to know one another as the adults we are now. It'll give us a stronger foundation to start on than when we were just two crazy, hormonal kids."

I held her tighter and placed a kiss on the top of her head. It was unfortunate that she still over-processed her hair with all the dyes, but nothing could be done for that.

"Why didn't you ever have kids?"

"The right man to have them with got away." She shrugged as she insinuated that I was the one who should have fathered her children. I couldn't and wouldn't feel bad about that or the fact that I had my children with another woman. "My husband was a convenience and neither of us were too inclined to bring children into the mix."

"Do you regret it?" I asked. "I'm guessing that ship has already sailed now."

"There isn't a chance for me to have them biologically any longer," she admitted, though she didn't seem too torn up over the fact.

"You good with that, or would you want to try for adoption or something?"

"No. I'm good with it. I made my peace years ago and I don't mind having all that extra time with you. Call me selfish, but we waited this long to get our second chance, I want it to be just us."

"I do still have grown kids and a grand baby in my life. So, it won't always be just us."

She tucked her head into my chest, so I couldn't see her face, but there was no missing the way her body froze up for a second either. "Yeah, I know all that. It's fine. It's not like they're around twenty-four-seven the way it would be if they were children."

"That's true."

CHAPTER 12
TRIPP -A MONTH LATER

"ARE you ready to celebrate with me tonight?" June asked as soon as I picked up her call.

"What are we celebrating?" I was going through recent receipts for the bar in the clubhouse as I waited for her to fill me in. It seemed like the men were drinking less these days. That in itself might have been worth celebrating if it didn't feel like shit was about to hit the fan. That weird feeling in my gut was almost never wrong, and I'd learned to pay heed and keep aware when it hit me.

"Freedom," June answered cryptically.

"Okay, I'll be there in about an hour to get you."

"Can we take one of your motorcycles?" she asked in such a deceptively sweet voice that I had to stop and think about it.

"You remember what I told you about being on the back of my bike?"

"I remember. I think it's time."

"But you're still..."

She cut me off. "We're celebrating my freedom tonight, Tripp." It finally clued in what 'freedom' meant.

"How?"

June giggled. "He filed for divorce a month ago when I talked to him about it. He seemed happier than a clam to do it too." That last bit had a bitter note to it, but that wasn't something I'd get into over the phone with June.

"Okay, well wear some sturdy clothing then. Jeans, closed toe shoes, leather jacket if you have one. I'll have to stop and grab a new helmet for you."

"You don't have an extra?"

"No. The only extra I keep laying around is for my daughter and she doesn't share helmets ever."

"I suppose, I can see her point there."

"Be around in about an hour to pick you up." I told her before hanging up. There was something about the way she said that last bit that made me tense. That same feeling in my gut hit me again. Something wasn't right. It was possible that I was projecting that feeling onto something completely innocuous said by June, but it wasn't something I was willing to ignore either.

When I threw my leg over my motorcycle and turned it on, I took a minute to imagine June on the back with me and my stomach knotted in on itself again. I wasn't ready, but considering June had finally freed herself from the husband that was holding us back from taking our friendship to the relationship level, it was the least I could do.

June and I got to the restaurant I picked to take her to. It couldn't be anything fancy, since it was her first time on the back of my bike, and she couldn't get dressed up. Still, I chose a decent place that I thought she'd be impressed with. We were just about to head inside when my phone started ringing. I glanced down to see it was Kip.

"Ignore it. We're here to celebrate," June demanded.

"It's my son. I can't ignore a call from my kids."

"They're adults," she huffed.

I narrowed my eyes on June as I answered the call right in front of her. "Hope this is important," I said into the phone before Kip could speak.

"Yeah, need you at Jared and Star's place. It's a fucking emergency. Get here yesterday." He hung up after delivering his message. I turned right back around headed for my motorcycle.

"Where are you going?"

"Emergency at my daughter's house. You can either get on the back of my bike and hold your questions for later, or you can call for a ride home."

I didn't miss the angry look she threw my way, but June made her way to the back of my bike, threw her leg over, and fastened her helmet back on her head quickly.

It only took a few minutes to get to Star and Bagger's place, but that might have had something to do with the speed I ran the whole way. June's heart was about to beat out of her chest by the time I pulled my motorcycle up at the curb.

"You could have killed us," she hissed at me as she yanked her helmet off.

"What part of emergency did you not understand?" I glanced up to see both of my kids and Jared standing in the doorway of the house. It didn't look like any of them were hurt, but then again I didn't see my grandson either. I yanked June's hand when she hesitated and tried to stay behind. "Come on," I ordered.

"This isn't the best time to reveal our relationship to them," she whisper-hissed to me.

"Too late for that now, since they already saw you on the back of my bike."

"What the hell is going on?" I yelled to my kids as I dropped my helmet and left it behind.

"You better come in and take a seat before we answer that." Star stated before she turned and left the door wide open for us to come through.

"You pregnant or something?"

"No, she isn't but your daughter is sick," Kip mentioned, but there was an undercurrent to his tone that set my hackles to rising.

June reached out to Star and held onto her, maybe a little too tightly, as she spoke. "I'm sorry to hear that honey. Let me know if there is anything I can do, okay?"

The offer was typical enough of what someone should say, but there was something about it that tripped my radar. June was not being sincere. The act she put on for my daughter was just that and it did not sit right with me. Before I could say anything, Kip started in.

"Do you remember Vina?"

"Yeah, used to work for the club," I answered cryptically. There was no way in hell that June would take kindly to hearing exactly what capacity Vina had worked for the club previously.

"She had a daughter. She's just a month younger than Knox," Kip went on to say.

"Fuck! Did you knock her up?" I asked as my guts twisted at the thought. If my son got the woman I'd been secretly pining for pregnant, I wouldn't know how to handle that shit.

"No, apparently you did," Kip growled back.

"I – What?" I shook my head, as if to clear the cobwebs that must be there. "What the fuck did you just say?"

June gasped and took several noticeable steps away from me. I moved closer and wrapped my arm around her waist all while maintaining eye contact with my son. Kip pulled out some paperwork and handed it to me.

"I took a test when Bagger told me that she was claiming the kid might be his."

"What on Earth would you take a test for?" June asked Kip and I knew the minute he answered, everything would change. Truthfully, everything had already changed anyway, if what my son said was the truth. There was no way I'd leave Vina swinging in the wind if she had my kid. I also knew from experience that June wouldn't stick around to be a part of that whether I was with the kid's mom or not.

"All of us were potential baby daddies, since Vina was a club girl."

"A club girl?" June's face immediately drained of color when she realized the implications there. My son and I were both potentially the father of the baby along with several of our club brothers. Kip didn't bother to give her more of an explanation and instead turned his attention back to me and nodded toward the papers he placed in my hand moments ago.

"That test says I'm not the father, but that I am related to her. That puts you on the hook," Kip explained as I finally turned my attention to the DNA results on the paper he had handed me.

"Why are we just finding out about this kid if she's the same age as Knox? That's what? Eight months now?"

"Seven," Star corrected.

"Tripp?" June questioned. "This isn't true."

"Fuck!" I huffed out before looking away from the papers and giving June my attention. "That was when I saw you out with Barry."

It killed me to see June standing in front of my kids crying about another pregnancy that would most likely keep us apart. It was as though history was repeating itself. "It looks like I'll forever be punished for that mistake."

"No offense, lady, but I think there are bigger things to talk about here than your hurt feelings," Breakneck snapped at her. It was the first time I realized he was even in the room.

"Excuse me," June gasped.

"What the fuck, Break?" I stood there ready to hand my enforcer his ass, but then his next words nearly doubled me over as if he had been the one to strike out at me physically.

"Your kid has cancer, man. That's what we brought you here to tell you. She needs a bone marrow donation. Star was tested, she's a half match to the kid. Don't know about Kip yet. I'm guessing you won't be enough of a match based on what I know about that shit, so that won't matter. But Vina's been doing this shit alone, brother. I think maybe you need to worry about that woman's drama later," Breakneck said, pointing to June who was openly sobbing in front of all of us. "Worry about helping your daughter and her momma out instead."

"Fuck!" I roared. "She's a baby. How is she sick?"

"Cancer doesn't care, man." Breakneck moved closer and grasped my shoulder to offer me support. I'd been ready to drop from the shock and honestly didn't know whether to knock him off or fall to my fucking feet. I went with option three and pulled him in for a hug because I needed someone to lean on in that moment and fuck, I needed to hide the damn tears that spilled from my eyes at the thought of having a daughter who was so fucking sick that she needed a bone marrow transplant to survive.

"Break, why don't you get June home for us. I think we have some things to discuss as a family and I'm not sure she wants to be here for this." Star ordered.

"Don't you dare try to send me away," June shouted at my daughter as she stood with an angry fist in the air, pointing an accusatory finger at Star for some fucking reason. "None of this is your business."

"You need to sit the fuck down, lady. Tripp is my father. That baby is my sister. And you are absolutely nothing. He hasn't put a fucking ring on your finger or his colors on your back, so you can fuck right on off with that attitude."

"Star!" I bellowed. "This was big news to hear. Have a little fucking heart."

"You know what, Dad? You're the one who has been

keeping whatever the two of you have going on a secret, so if you want to blame anyone for how that shit just went down, go look in a mirror."

"You are a disrespectful brat."

"You're standing in my mother fucking house!" Jared reminded June. "You will not speak to my woman that way."

"Get out!" Star pointed to the direction of the front door. "He's right. Our family is in crisis and the last thing we need is for you to stand here and pretend that everything happening is all about you."

June took one menacing step toward my daughter when I called her off. "June!"

"Don't be angry with me because I'm his daughter. He was married to my mother." Star spouted before I could deescalate the situation.

"He was supposed to be married to me then!" She turned her hateful glare on my son. "But your mother got knocked up with you conveniently when Tripp and I were having a fight. He was my fiancé back then. She stole him away. Now, history is repeating itself again."

My face drained of all the blood that had been in it. In all her anger, June had just outed herself as the other woman in my life before I met Kim. My kids had heard stories about her from their mother and uncle when they were growing up. They knew the truth. Because they knew the truth of our history, I didn't think they would take too kindly to June being welcomed back into my life. She would be a constant reminder of their mother and how we wouldn't have been a family if June had gotten her way.

"June, you need to go. I'll come find you once I know everything. We'll talk then."

"No." In the most literal sense of putting her foot down about something, June stomped at me. "Either you leave here with me now, or that's it, we're done. I won't come in second to your children you had with some whore again."

Jared grabbed Star just as she launched herself toward June. "Call my mother a whore again, you fucking cunt! I will kill you! I will fucking gut your sorry ass!"

"Holy shit!" Breakneck called out. "Shoulda taught baby girl how to ride. She could have been an enforcer too."

"Get the fuck out, June." I yelled at the woman who just today had become free to date me in the way we had been working toward for months – years, if you counted our shared history.

"You can't be serious. I left Barry for you."

"Maybe you should have stayed with him. You're not the same woman I used to know. The woman I once knew would never have spoken to my children that way or demanded to be elevated above them."

"They ruined my life!" she screamed at me.

"No, *I* did that. I screwed up and ruined what we had. That was on me, not them. You will not put that blame anywhere other than where it belongs." I thumped my chest twice to indicate where the blame lie. "Right here. Now, leave before we end things on an even worse note. You made your choice, go on."

"Tripp," June whimpered out my name. Then she stepped back as if I'd slapped her. Maybe I had with the fierce look I'd thrown her way.

"My daughter is sick. She's going to need me right now. You're not going to agree with that choice, so there's no point in having this argument."

June turned and stomped out of the house. Breakneck followed behind her, because as my enforcer, it was his job to see to any threats to our family. In that moment, June was a fucking threat.

"I never intended for the two of you to know," I said to my kids.

"How did you think that would work? You've been dating her again for how long?" I asked.

"Two years, except the time when I saw her out with her husband."

"Her husband?" he nodded. "Holy shit, what the hell? You know what? Never mind. I don't even want to know what you were thinking. You need to get in touch with Davina about everything. She got a copy of all three DNA test results, so she knows that Kip is a relative, which leaves you as the father. Let her know that I would like to meet my sister sometime soon." I nodded at Star.

"It sounds like you're kicking me out." I made a joke of it, but in all honesty, that's what it felt like.

"I am," Star agreed, much to my surprise. "You need to leave because I'm so infuriated with you right now, the things I want to say will do permanent damage."

I hung my head, knowing I deserved it. There was no getting around the fact that I'd screwed up by ever enter-taining the thought that I could have a healthy relationship with June. My kids would have never allowed that, and if I was honest with myself, that was exactly the reason I'd kept it quiet until it blew up in my face.

"I'll be angry with him later. Right now, he needs someone to be there for him." Kip called back to his sister as he followed me out of her house.

CHAPTER 13
TRIPP

THE SWEET, subtle perfume Davina wore tickled my senses, making me wish I could move in closer to her and inhale the delicate aroma. It was partly her mixed in with that perfume that I found so intriguing.

Until the night I found out about my daughter, I would have sworn I was over the beautiful woman who slipped through my fingertips thanks to my inability to act. Not being able to have her was why it was so easy for me to dive back through history and try again with June, despite knowing that we had reached our inevitable end back when we were in high school and certainly when I saw her out canoodling with the husband she supposedly didn't give a shit about.

She had almost fooled me into believing she could handle seeing my adult children that I'd had with Kim all those years ago. Her acceptance of the fact that I was still in the club, running it even, and that they were my family and weren't going anywhere was something else.

After the way she exploded on everyone, including my daughter, when she found out that Davina's daughter was mine as well... I didn't see how anything could be salvageable there. Then again, considering my reaction to Davina versus the one I didn't really have with June, I think my body had already been telling me what my mind wouldn't clue into. The past - at least the one concerning June - should stay exactly there.

"I just want you to be prepared," Davina's voice immediately pulled me out of my thoughts of the other woman. "She's small and it is heartbreaking to see her hooked up to everything."

I nodded and swallowed down my anxiety. If Davina had been handling everything on her own where our daughter was concerned, then I'd step up and do my part too - even if that meant keeping a smile on my face when all I wanted to do was rage and fucking tear the world down for being a place where small children could get sick like this.

"It'll be okay. Whatever I see in there won't scare me away, if that's what you're worried about. If anything, it's going to solidify my place in your lives."

She simply shrugged her shoulders and put her hand on the door, ready to push it open. It was obvious by her response that she didn't believe I'd be there when all was said and done. That just went to show that she didn't know me very well.

"This isn't like it was with your children. We're not together and our daughter is sick." Tears pooled in Davina's eyes as she tried to make me understand. "She might not make it. I hope and pray every day that she does, but the truth is, her body is so tiny, and it has to fight this giant monster, Tripp. She might not..."

"We're going to do everything possible to give her one hell of a fighting chance, Vina. I promise, you will never be alone in this again. If I'd known sooner, you wouldn't have been alone for any of it."

"Are you angry with me?"

"No. I understand why you didn't bother to tell anyone until now. You weren't sure who the father was and the odds that it might have been someone like Breakneck would have kept me quiet, too," I teased. Vina rolled her eyes at me, but the smile that tipped up the corners of her mouth was everything. Something told me that she probably hadn't had any good reason to smile lately.

"We better go in, so I can introduce you to your daughter before she's too tired."

I followed Vina into the hospital room where our little girl was in a crib with monitors attached to her little toes along with an IV. The quiet beeps from the machine were the only sound in the otherwise still room as the sweet face with blue-gray eyes that looked just like mine stared up at me. "She's so small," I muttered before moving closer.

"Hey there, baby girl. I'm your daddy and we're going to do our best to make sure you get healthy enough to get out of here."

The sweet thing smiled up at me as if she knew exactly the promise I was making. I only hoped like hell it was one that could be kept.

"Coral, I love you, my sweetness," Davina murmured to

her as she leaned in and dropped a kiss to the gaunt cheeks that should be puffed up with baby fat.

The moment I stood over the crib and leaned in so that I could touch the hollowed-out cheeks of my baby girl, my heart melted. It wasn't like being introduced to my other children for the first time when they were born. Even though they had been tiny little humans, there was nothing but hope and bright futures shining back at me from their little eyes. Coral was fragile in a way my other two children never had been.

Coral reached her hand up and took hold of my pinky finger. I allowed her to guide my hand closer to her middle where she continued to hold on like she knew exactly who I was, despite the fact that it was my first time meeting her.

"Hi baby girl," I whispered. The tired smile she beamed at me in response was everything. "You are so beautiful." The words slipped free of me before I even understood what I was saying. "You and your momma aren't going to have to worry about anything ever again."

I glanced up to see Davina swiping at a tear on her face. "Sorry," she whispered.

I crooked my finger, gesturing her to come to me. When Davina got close enough, I wrapped my arm around her waist and held her tight to my side while our daughter held onto the fingers of my other hand. "Not kidding, Vina. The two of you don't have to worry about anything anymore."

"I-Um, well, I don't really know what to say to that."

Our baby girl closed her eyes and drifted off, so I pulled Vina down to sit with me in the chair by her bedside.

"I want you to tell me everything, starting with the day

we spoke when you were leaving. Did you know you were pregnant then?"

She nodded her head and then glanced at our daughter again. "If I'd known she was yours, I would have told you."

I shook my head. "I'm not angry about that, Vina. I understand why you took off. No matter who the father was, the club would have taken care of you, if you had told me. Hell, the fact that you've been going through all of this and never said a word..." I shook my head once more. "I just can't wrap my head around it. Did you have anyone with you when you had her?"

"No. It was just me and some super kind nurses who got me through it."

"Fuck," I hissed. "That makes me feel like a complete failure."

"Why? It's not like you knew and chose not to show up."

"I should have known. I was there when Kim had Kip and Star. What that woman went through to give birth to them," I started to say before turning my eyes back to Vina's. They were swimming in tears that she was trying her best to hold back. "I wish like hell we could go back, so that I could be there for you, for both of you, from the very beginning."

Vina heaved out a heavy sigh and nodded her head. "I'm sure if you could have one wish granted, our daughter wouldn't even be here."

"That's not fair."

"No, but it is true, and I would be so happy for you if you could have your wife back."

"Okay, how about we put away the wishes for any alternate past because it's not going down a road I think is healthy. I want you to fill me in on everything that I've missed, including why some prick doctor out there was giving me a look that almost landed my fist in his face."

Vina's shoulder's slumped as she turned her eyes toward the door. "I'm assuming you saw the worst doctor in the world. Dr. Markham was the one that had social services come take our daughter from me after I brought her into the hospital about bruises that kept popping up on her when I put her down to sleep."

"He did what?"

I spent the next few minutes listening to her describe in detail everything the nurse, doctor, and that bitch from social services had put her and our daughter through. I made a silent vow to make them all pay. No one fucked with my family and got away with it.

"I know that look," Vina announced.

"What look?"

"The one you guys get on your face when you're about to fuck up someone's world." I cocked a brow at her as if to say, "And?" her sighed response along with the droop in her shoulders, as if she felt defeated by my actions, stopped me in my tracks.

"What?"

"I need you to put a pin in it."

"In what?"

"In whatever revenge scheme you're cooking up against those three. I understand because there is no cell in my body that doesn't want to bury them all myself, but you can't do anything right now."

"Why the fuck not?"

"Who do you think would be the prime suspect if something were to happen to them?" she asked as her thumb pointed back to herself. "This girl. Not you. Not the club. Me. I cannot lose my daughter again. It's bad enough they've told me to be prepared for the possibility of losing my daughter forever anyway. I would never forgive you if her last moments on this earth had to be spent amongst strangers wondering why her momma forgot about her."

"Fuck." The word blew free of me on a whisper. "You have my word that I will not make things harder on the two of you. We'll focus on getting our girl healthy again. Then, we'll bring her home, and after enough time has passed, they'll get what's coming to them. I swear they won't get away with what they've done."

"My lawyer is already working on making them pay."

"Losing some money isn't enough of a punishment."

Vina shook her head. "He's going after all their credentials too."

"Good. Once that is over, I'll go after whatever is left." She nodded her agreement that time and we both sat in silence a while and watched our daughter sleep.

"I was scared," I admitted as we sat there surrounded by the hushed noises in the hallways.

"When you found out about Coral?"

"That too, but I'm talking about when I left you alone in my bed." She gasped and turned to look at me before quickly diverting her eyes back to our daughter.

"Maybe we shouldn't talk about that," Vina suggested.

"No, I think it's long past time we talked about it. Had I done that instead of letting other shit get in my head, you never would have gone through everything alone. So, we're going to do this before any more time is wasted."

I held onto Davina as I explained the year-long crush I harbored on her, the months I spent getting to know my high school ex-girlfriend again. The pivotal moment between June and me back then that sent me into a bit of a tailspin and questioning my own judgement. Then, I worked my way to the night we spent together.

"I'd been wanting you for so long, fantasizing about being with you."

"Tripp," she huffed in a desperate plea to get me to shut up about our time together.

"No, you need to hear this as much as I need to say it. I wanted you. Fuck, that never went away."

"You've been dating someone else, that lady."

I nodded my head and continued to explain my history with June over the past two years and how we had never been intimate. I also explained why I walked away from Vina after our night together.

"I get that you didn't want to have star come home and be blindsided. Plus, I was never enough considering I was a club girl."

"No, that didn't have anything to do with it." She gave me a sidelong glance that all but called me out on my bull-shit. "Okay, it had a little to do with it, but only because of my son. I didn't know if the two of you had ever hooked up before. You were around before he started dating Scout, so there was no way to be sure without asking."

"I had not been with him before you. He, um, after... I couldn't really tell him no."

"I understand that."

"It was just the one time. I hated it because Scout was my friend and it felt like I was betraying both you and her."

"You could have refused him."

She nodded her head. "I could have, but I needed a little more time before I had enough money to leave."

"You were planning to leave even before you found out you were pregnant?"

"Yes," she answered hesitantly. "Our conversation, the one we had that night, you made a good point. I needed to figure out what I wanted to do with my life. I think I was the oldest club girl at the time, so it made sense that my time with the club would be coming to an end sooner than later."

"What the hell are you talking about? Jesus, woman, your age doesn't mean shit. You're fucking drop dead gorgeous, you have a bangin' body, and it's all packaging for the sweetness you have inside that draws every motherfucker with a swinging dick your way."

"Oh!"

"Oh!" I repeated mockingly. "It seems like we both let shit get in our heads that had no need to be there. Fuck, I feel like an idiot."

"You shouldn't. You were putting your children first and that is admirable. They're so lucky to have you as their father."

I squeezed Vina's waist and pulled her down so that her upper body wasn't sitting up and stiff and instead leaned against mine. "No more miscommunications and irrational fears, Vina. I'm here for you, for our daughter, and once she gets better that still won't change."

"Okay, Tripp."

"Promise, sweetheart."

"Thank you," she whispered. It didn't take long for her breaths to even out. My woman was worn the fuck down by the shit hand she'd been dealt and the fact that she had been left to navigate everything practically on her own. That shit was about to change because I couldn't walk away again without claiming her.

CHAPTER 14
JUNE

I REGRETTED my reaction to hearing that Tripp may have fathered another child with yet another whore attached to the club. First, it was Kim. Now, some other whore - truly a whore this time - had gotten pregnant by him. Not only that, but apparently the little shit-stain was sick.

It was bad enough I'd have to deal with the grown adult children he had with that pile of ashes he still called his wife, but now, there was a new woman.

I watched them together. Her t-shirt spread tightly across her perky breasts to entice him. "Once a whore, always a whore," I mumbled out loud to no one.

The blonde hair on her head appeared natural rather than the dye job I had to maintain since my mom pushed me to change it from my original boring brown in high school. I had a better hair stylist these days, but years of chemicals and upkeep made it too course to flow freely around my shoulders in a silky waterfall the way hers did.

Heat bloomed from somewhere deep inside my belly

where I stored up all my hate as I watched the way Tripp looked at her. Of course, he thought she was beautiful, the little slut was probably the same age as his daughter. Half our age. Everything was still tight and fresh on her body despite the fact that she'd already spit out a child. Who knew, maybe there were more. Maybe her body was ravaged under her clothing. I could only hope.

Mine was still pristine in that I had no stretch marks or obvious signs of pregnancy that most women my age carried around. Everything I had was still mostly firm, though I'd allowed myself to get a bit doughy over the last couple years in spots. I went for regular Botox to keep the wrinkles at bay, but there were places where they couldn't be hidden well, no matter how hard I tried.

No matter what I did - there was no way to look like a 20-something buxom blonde club whore. And I couldn't compete for time with a sick kid either.

I'd just have to make sure the sick kid isn't part of the equation for much longer. Then, I can be the shoulder he cries on. It wouldn't take much convincing to have him blame the bitch for keeping his kid from him until she was too sick to live, and I'll feed right into that for him.

I grinned as I got out of the car and followed them into the hospital. The hat I wore, along with the oversized sunglasses and coat would keep them from noticing me long enough to find out where the kid was being kept.

"Can I help you?"

It startled me to discover the nurse who asked the question was speaking to me. I shook my head, but she stayed there, tapping her foot impatiently at me. "This floor is only for family who are visiting."

"Just trying to get the nerve up to go see her," I explained while trying to look as miserable about that as possible.

She eyed me with a look of disbelief, but I didn't really care. "Who exactly are you here to see?"

I shook my head and sniffled as I bowed my head and pretended to be overwhelmed with emotion. Truthfully, I'd already seen which room that bitch had taken Tripp to. I'd also seen what looked like a tender moment pass between them before that happened. The rage I kept hidden deep inside me flared to life again as he professed that that whore would never be alone again.

I saw history repeating itself.

He was mine.

He would remain mine.

I waited too long to get Kim out of the picture. That wouldn't be the case this time. This time, I'd start with the kid and make sure the whore followed quickly behind her.

"I just need a restroom to freshen up before I go in," I told the nosy ass nurse as I walked away. There was no point in me staying there longer. Instead, I headed back down and wait to follow Tripp to wherever he went next. Then again, maybe I should follow the whore instead...

Decisions, Decisions.

"Ma'am, I'm going to have to ask you to leave this floor if you can't tell me who you're here to see." When I turned around to tell the nurse to go fuck herself, she had a phone held up and took a picture of me. Unfortunately, I'd had my glasses pulled off my face, and she got the full shot. Damn. At least I hadn't told her I was there for Tripp or to see the kid - whose name I couldn't remember.

I didn't bother responding to her and left immediately. My cousin was a nurse at the hospital. All the information I needed to know would eventually come from her, since she had access. Anna didn't need to know why I needed the information, just that I had an interest. Maybe, I could trust her with just enough to tell her that all I wanted was to help Tripp out and make sure he had everything he needed for his new baby. She wasn't the brightest of girls when we were growing up together, so the chances of her putting two-and-two together when the staff discovered the kid dead one day would be minuscule.

Besides, it wasn't like she'd be able to turn me in. She would be considered an accessory to murder if she tried after giving me all the information needed to commit the crime.

CHAPTER 15
TRIPP - 3 DAYS LATER

"Tripp Martin?"

I turned to see a woman standing there that looked vaguely familiar, but I couldn't place her. She obviously knew me since she called me by my full name.

"Yeah," I answered and stood waiting for her to catch up to me.

She huffed and puffed as she finally made the final step to close the distance between us. "Sorry, I tried to catch you before you left the floor where your daughter is, but the elevator door closed too quickly."

"Is something wrong with Coral?" I asked. My heart ticked up a few beats as I wondered what could have changed in the time I'd walked downstairs to go grab a drink for Vina and myself.

"You don't remember who I am, do you?"

"Can't say as I do."

"Right. Well, I'm June's cousin. Anna."

"That's why you seemed a little familiar." I nodded at her. "So, this isn't about Coral then?"

"No. I mean yes. Look, I don't know. There's something I needed to tell you, and Jesus there's no easy way to do this."

"I find just spitting things out helps the situation and relieves the tension."

The woman nodded and swallowed hard, like it almost hurt to do so. "June came to me a couple days ago wanting information." I nodded while waiting for her to say more. "She wanted to know about your daughter, what she was in the hospital for, what type of treatments she was receiving, and a whole slew of other questions. She claimed it was simply because she was concerned as the two of you are dating again."

"We were until the day I found out I had a daughter and that she was in the hospital. June said a few horrible things to me and my other kids. I haven't spoken to her since that day. I'm not sure why she would want information about a child I just found out about."

"That's the thing that worries me. She wanted me to give her all that information." She stumbled over her words quickly to assure me that it never happened. "I didn't tell her anything and when I refused, she demanded that I help her gain access to Coral's room."

"She did what?" I yelled angrily.

"I didn't do that either, but I thought you should know because it's not okay for her to do that. I won't help her, but I'm worried because she seemed really determined and one of the other nurses has been showing a picture around to everyone on that floor. I'm fairly certain it was my cousin, and she was on the floor where your daughter is. That was a few days before she came to me asking questions."

"I need to get back up there. I just left Vina and my daughter alone." Panic hit and I started running as I pulled my phone out and dialed the clubhouse. "Get Scout on the line, I need her." The demand was past my lips before the prospect who answered could even offer up the usual greeting.

It took me no time to get back upstairs to check on my girls. When I found Davina nodding off in a chair next to our daughter's crib, I quietly made my way back to the nurse's station and gave them a picture of June.

"This woman should not be allowed on the floor at all, but definitely not near my daughter. If you see her, I want a phone call immediately and security better handle business before I get here."

"That's the woman I saw lurking around a few days ago," one of them said. I turned to her, and she pulled her phone out to show me a picture of June in an oversized coat, a floppy hat, and large sunglasses dangling from her fingers.

"I'm so sorry. I didn't know who she was trying to get to. I asked who she was here to see, but she tried some fake crying stunt, like she needed to pull herself together before she went in to see whoever she was supposedly here to visit. When I questioned her again, she took off for the bathroom or something, but I called out to her and was able to snap this picture. I circulated it with the nurses because she seemed suspicious, but I didn't think to show our patients or their families." The nurse seems lost in thought for a minute before speaking again. "Come to think of it, she showed up not long after you and Coral's mother did that day."

"Thanks for letting me know."

I walked away because I knew the nurse didn't mean anything by forgetting to let us know. She had simply been overwhelmed with work and then forgot. That was life and there was no reason to point out to her that her inaction could have gotten someone killed. Especially since I didn't think June had it in her to do that. She was probably just curious about the woman and child who would make it impossible for us to be together again like she wanted.

Part of me felt a little bad about it, since she had finally divorced her husband. The other part thought I was setting her free to go find true happiness elsewhere. It wasn't something she could find with me. That much had become evident before we even found out about my daughter.

At that point, June hadn't met my kids yet because she kept claiming she wasn't ready. But considering the low-level of anger that seemed to radiate from her and the pure fire in her eyes if I even mentioned my late wife, it was clear it would always be a problem. She could claim that she'd put our history behind us, but she lost me to Kim when my late wife got pregnant with Kip. The resentment over what Kim and I did obviously rubbed off on Kip in her eyes and was pushed onto my daughter when Star came along as well.

Instead of heading back to the hospital room where my

baby girl and her mom were resting, I called the clubhouse again. They hadn't been able to find Scout and for some fucking reason or other I didn't have her cell phone number. That was something that needed fixing, especially since she was our Tech Officer now. It was a new position we created for her – like a Sgt. At Arms but on the digital side of things.

"Did you find her?" I barked into the phone when the prospect picked up.

"Yeah, she thought it sounded urgent and is headed to you along with Kip, Star, and Bagger."

"Fuck, whole family reunion, huh?" I grumbled as I hung up. It was probably a good thing. This way, Davina would know that she was family, and we all had her back. We would always have Coral's back, no matter what, as well.

Just as I moved from the waiting room back out to the hall, I heard the nurses trying to stop my family from coming down to see us. "It's okay. Those are my children," I called out to them.

"Ballsy fucking nurses," Bagger complained.

I shook my head. "They did their job. When I tell you why, you'll understand and thank them for being ballsy enough to go up against bikers wearing their cuts."

"What the fuck is going on?" Kip asked.

"Come with me back to the waiting room. Don't want Vina overhearing this and worrying."

Kip grinned at me like the little shit he still was, even though he was a full-grown man now. "Vina, huh?"

"Shut it," Star demanded as she slapped the back of her brother's head while Scout and Bagger looked on in amusement.

"Why were you trying to get a hold of me?" Scout asked as we all finally made our way into the room and closed the door.

"June, my ex-girlfriend from high school," I told her. "Need all the information you can get on her and what she's been up to all this time, and I need a tail on her. She showed up a few days ago on the floor, apparently followed me here and then followed Vina and me upstairs."

"I'm sure she was just curious, considering this is the second time you having a surprise kid ruined things between the two of you," Star groused. She wasn't happy with me for the way I carried myself when I was still a kid, or for the way I had kept June hidden for so long this time. She felt that if I had just forced June to interact with her and Kip, that the woman would have gotten over her hesitancy about them.

Maybe she was right, but something wasn't sitting well with me now that I knew she'd been following me around. Who was to say it was a one-time thing?

"Her cousin came to see me today. She wanted to warn me that June asked for her help to get up on this floor and into Coral's room. She also asked for all her medical information."

"What the fuck?" Bagger and Kip both said at once as Scout scrunched her nose up while tapping away on her phone.

"Dad," Star called to me hesitantly. "You don't think she'd hurt my sister, do you?" My stomach clenched with the fear that she might just.

"I have no way of knowing, baby, but this is the second time a woman with a surprise kid of mine has caused a rift -

in June's eyes. There's no telling how a woman would take that."

"I'm having Breakneck go through security feeds for the past couple weeks. Bagger, he needs your access to check the ones outside your house," Scout insisted.

"You good here?" Bagger asked Star.

"Yeah, go help him. Let me know what you find. I'm going to stay here with my sister and Davina." My eldest daughter turned to look at me then. "If you need to leave to try to go confront June, I'll stick close to the girls."

"Thanks baby girl, I appreciate it." I kissed her forehead, same as her man did before he took off.

"I'm going to stick around, too. Make sure someone from the club is always here watching out for them."

I nodded to my son, proud as fuck that my kids embraced my daughter and her mother rather than causing problems because of her age or anything else.

"Find that bitch and figure out what she's up to. We won't tolerate her messing with family. If you need a female to bitch slap her around for information, I'll be glad to come in and do it."

Scout laughed at Star. "Don't worry, they have me as the tech officer-slash-cyber enforcer, but it also means I get the wet work when it comes to females," she teased with a wink.

"That's not funny, Scout," Kip called out to her.

"Didn't ask for your opinion," she sassed back over her shoulder as she left the room.

"When are you going to straighten things out with your woman?" I asked my son once she was gone.

"As soon as she makes me stop paying for my past

mistakes." He sighed and left the waiting room with his sister and me following.

"Hopefully, you two don't wait too much longer to patch things up. Life's short. You know that better than most." Kip agreed with a slight incline of his head to acknowledge what I meant. His mother was taken from us far too soon. You just never knew what would happen.

Davina popped her head out into the hallway about the time we came even with the door to the room where my daughter was being treated. "Hey, I thought I saw Bagger and Scout go by."

"They had to go do something for me. I'm needed too, for club business, but Star and Kip are going to hang out with their sister, if that's okay with you."

She seemed almost uncertain at first, but then nodded her head. I leaned in and kissed her cheek before whispering in her ear. "They aren't sticking around to give you a hard time about anything. They're genuinely concerned about their sister."

A blush warmed her cheeks as she took a step back and opened the door for my kids to get through. "I'll see you and my little peanut in a bit," I told her before I placed a quick kiss on her lips and left.

BEFORE I COULD GET BACK to the clubhouse, Scout was already blowing up my phone. The news wasn't great either.

"She's been following Davina, you, and even Star for quite some time. We caught her on video outside Bagger's house even before you took her there. She was watching them, Prez. I don't like how this is shaping up."

"Do you think she's been doing it the whole time?"

"As in since you were in high school or since you ran into one another again?" Scout asked and it made me think.

"What if she's been doing it the whole time?"

"I'll look into things and see if we can go back further, but you know, it's probably going to be impossible to tell how long this has been going on. Even video surveillance has its time limitations. Most videos are dumped after a set time unless something notable happened."

"Do your best and keep someone on her six. I don't want her out of our sight if we can help it."

"On it," Scout agreed before hanging up.

CHAPTER 16
DAVINA

Tripp kissed me. He kissed me on the lips in front of his grown children. It took a minute for the shock to wear off and my discomfort to show in front of Kip and Star. It was the first time I'd been around them when their father showed me any kind of affection and then he simply left me there to deal with the fallout.

"Stop staring at us like we're going to rip your head off," Star insisted.

"Is Coral awake?" Kip asked. I turned my attention away from his sister and back to him as I shook my head. For some reason, it was easier to interact with Kip.

Maybe it was easier with Kip because I was used to dealing with all the club brothers, or perhaps because I knew him intimately. Actually, thinking about the one incident made it awkward again. I wouldn't tell Tripp, because he wouldn't appreciate hearing the details, even if they might make him feel better. I honestly never thought Kip was a strong contender as Coral's father because he never even finished with me. The poor man, he felt guiltier than hell over what he was doing and why. He essentially used me to make one woman jealous and to piss off the other one. I wouldn't want to be in his shoes and hated that he put me in the middle of his shit, but in the end, he couldn't follow through anyway. Not that anyone but the two of us knew that.

"She went down about fifteen minutes ago, but y'all can still go in and sit with her. The way the meds have her all over the place, she might wake up again in a few minutes or she could be out for a couple hours." I lifted my shoulders in a semblance of a shrug before blowing out a long breath and sagging a bit.

To my complete surprise, Star came and wrapped her arms around me. "Come on, let's get in there in case she wakes up. We can have a quiet conversation while she sleeps and hopefully put your mind at ease about a few things."

"Okay." My muttered acquiescence was ignored as we all filed into my daughter's private room. We all moved to the far corner of the room where there was a small couch, chair, and table. I fidgeted nervously, picking at my nails as the siblings got comfortable. Kip, who took the seat beside me, reached over and stilled my hands by putting his on top of mine.

"There is no need to be this nervous around us."

"How can you say that? I had a child with your father and didn't tell anyone."

"You didn't know he was the father," Kip mentioned.

"It could have been you, too," I stupidly reminded him. He smirked at me because we both knew it was the least probable scenario and why. It was Star who cleared her throat to get my attention that caught me off guard since Kip's only response was that dumb half-assed grin.

Star rolled her eyes at her brother. "I'm not even going to discuss how gross it is to think of you and Dad dipping your dicks in the same pussy ponds."

"Pussy ponds?" Kip couldn't even repeat the words without bursting out into laughter which made me giggle as well. Ice thoroughly broken, Star winked at me and then leaned forward to place her hand on top of mine and her brother's.

"First, you need to know we all understand. Heaven forbid, that beautiful girl could have had Breakneck as a father, and I don't blame you one bit for running rather than finding out the truth." Once again, we all had a bit of a laugh at that. Breakneck wasn't a bad guy. He just wasn't someone any of us could see pinned down as a father.

"I don't know. The way he's been with my nanny, I think Breakneck might surprise us all."

"Maybe if he could stop fucking other women behind her back." Star sassed at her brother. It looked as though Kip was about to argue that Breakneck was not doing that shit, but Star cut him off. "The women at the club talk too much. Don't try to tell me that I'm wrong. He better get his shit together before that sweet girl hauls ass for good."

Star turned her attention back to me after setting Kip straight. "We're all here now. The truth is out there and the main focus for all of us is to make sure we do everything we can to give Coral her best fighting chance."

I nodded at that and swiped away the tears that fell in

response. Even though I had come to grips with my daughter's diagnosis, it was still a gut-punch response to think about her having to fight for her life at such a young age.

"Davina," Star called out pulling me back to the conversation.

"Yeah? Sorry, it's just..." I freed my hand from theirs to rub over my stomach. "Most of the time, I'm kind of numb to what's going on, but then I get this kick to the belly response when someone else brings me back to reality. I hate this. I hate that my baby is fighting so hard to stay with us and there is literally nothing I can do to help her."

"You're here for her. That's something."

"That's nothing. It's what I would be doing anyway. God!" I moaned. "If I could give her my life, my blood, my soul, whatever could keep her alive, healthy, and happy, I would."

Kip slid his arm around my shoulder and pulled me into his side where I promptly wet the sleeve of his shirt with tears I didn't even realize were falling.

"You're a good mother, Davina. You're here with her, giving her everything you can. Plus, you went looking for her father, even though it had to be a scary thing for you to do. Neither of you are alone anymore. You have family beside you now. We're family." Star insisted. "That's the gist of what I wanted to tell you, or I guess make you understand." She smirked at me then. "Besides, it appears our dad is smitten with you just as much as he is with our little sister."

I shook my head, as if to deny the chemistry that I shared with their dad. We hadn't really discussed things between us yet. He promised to be there for my daughter and me and told me he'd basically been infatuated with me before but afraid to start something real. There was the kiss too, but I wasn't sure what to make of that.

"I don't think..."

"Do you know that I've never seen my dad kiss another woman if he knew I was around?" she asked.

"What do you mean?"

"I mean that he kissed you on the mouth in front of us, and the last woman he consciously did that with was our mother."

"That can't be right," I argued. "You were gone a long time, too."

"Oh, but it is true." Star turned to her brother then. "Have you seen it happen? You would know better than me, since you've been around the whole time I was gone."

"Nope. I've never seen him look at another woman the way he did our mother either, until today."

"Please, stop. I think you're reading things into the situation that aren't there. He's concerned because our daughter is sick, and we just recently had a conversation about everything Coral and I have been through."

"About that," Kip stated in a no-nonsense way that made the hair on the back of my neck stand on end. "I overheard a nurse talking out there about how you had your daughter taken away for abuse and how it delayed her getting the care she needed."

"I swear to you, I never abused my baby girl. It was all a misunderstanding because the cancer caused bruises that no one could explain. Since I'm a poor, single mother they decided that I must have..."

"Stop!" Star hissed at me. "We know." She stated emphatically. "We know you would never hurt our sister. I think what Kip was getting at is that we want you to explain to us why that happened, but more importantly who the hell accused you."

I tipped my head to the side in curiosity when I realized that their passionate responses aligned with the way their own father had acted when I told him my story. "I already told Tripp that nothing can happen right now. He's agreed to that."

"Why the hell would Dad agree to not seeking retribution on whoever was responsible for delaying medical care for his sick daughter?"

"He agreed because the first person they will point a finger at, if something were to happen to any of them, would be me."

We all sat quietly as they absorbed that information. "Fair point," Star finally conceded. "If I know my dad, though, he'll treat it as a dish best served cold."

Kip nodded his head. "Give it a little time and then go after the assholes. That's a good plan. We'll focus on getting Coral better first. She needs to be our priority right now, anyway."

I offered them both a small smile. "Thank you for understanding and for being here."

"It's what family does."

"Do you think I could bring Knox in to see Coral? She's his aunt, after all."

I couldn't contain the giggle that escaped me. "That's so weird. My daughter's nephew is older than her."

"Yeah, but cool at the same time," Kip agreed.

"I'll have to check with her doctor. Children carry so many germs that we're not even really aware of sometimes, especially if they're in daycare."

"Knox has a nanny and doesn't go out a lot, but I totally get erring on the side of caution. They can always meet later, when she's feeling better."

I nodded my head again and closed my eyes to imagine a day where my daughter got to meet her nephew who was so close in age to her. They could grow up as friends. At least I hoped for that outcome. I couldn't imagine a future where my baby girl didn't get to grow up like everyone else.

CHAPTER 17
TRIPP - 2 DAYS LATER

I WAS ABOUT to head back into the hospital to see my girls when my phone started ringing. "Whatcha got?"

"Are you at the hospital?" Scout asked.

"Yeah, just about to head back inside. I couldn't track the bitch down anywhere."

"Yeah, she's off the radar for now. We're looking though. I'm here, in the cafeteria. Can you meet me, so we can discuss what I found?"

"Be right there."

I hung up and took off into the hospital at a good clip and followed the signs to the cafeteria where I found Scout seated in the back corner, hunched over her laptop while dipping her fries in what looked like mayonnaise. That was nasty.

"What the fuck are you eating?"

She glanced down and then shrugged her shoulders before popping another white-sauce drenched fry into her mouth. "It's Ranch. They didn't have tartar sauce, which is what I prefer."

"You're fuckin' weird."

"You shouldn't knock it before you try it." She shoved her tray my way, but I shook my head.

"Pretty sure you didn't call me here to taste test your bullshit. What's up?"

All playfulness left her eyes as they met mine. Everything about her change in demeanor suddenly screamed how serious the shit was about to get.

"I don't know where she is right now, but I do know where she has been, and it isn't good."

"Fuck!" I groaned. "How did I not know she was up to shit?"

"Probably because you were living your life and not stuck up her ass 24-7." When I dropped a scathing look Scout's way, she grinned at me. "What? It's the truth. This broad is a bunny-boiler. It wouldn't surprise me to find out she's been tailing you and your whole family since high school."

My brows rose at that. "Are you serious?"

Scout nodded. "She is weirdly fixated on you and your family. I think we need to put security on your girls. Kip can handle his own shit. I know Star is capable, but she also has Bagger and he'll make sure she's safe once I give them the head's up as well. As for *Davina* and Coral, they need someone on them."

"They have me." I didn't miss the way Scout's face scrunched in displeasure when she said Davina's name.

"When you're not here?" she asked.

"I'll make sure someone is with them. What's your problem with Vina? I thought you two used to be friends."

"I thought so, too. Then I found out she wasn't sure if her daughter was Kip's."

"You can't hold that against her."

"I know," Scout huffed. "It doesn't mean that shit doesn't affect me. She slept with my boyfriend."

"You guys were broken up and she was a club girl. It was literally her job back then to go off with whatever man chose her for things. I think that's something you can understand, considering it's the reason you and Kip ended."

"You can't even say it, Prez. It bothers you too."

"Not in the way it bothers you. I'm telling you now, she's going to be around a lot. You need to get over it. You, of all people, should know the score. The only exception I ever made to the club girl rules of being available for every brother – no matter what – was for you. I did that for my son's sake. She didn't have the option to take an out when Kip was pissed off with you and Ash and came knocking on her door. I won't have you hold that against her. You want to hold it against my son for choosing to be with another woman – then do so. You will not give my woman a hard time about her past, though."

"Your woman?" Scout asked in a quiet tone.

"Most likely, if I can convince her to have me."

Scout's brows rose damn near into her hairline. "You're serious? You do know that people can coparent without being together in a relationship these days, right?"

"Smartass. Of course, I know that. The thing is, I had it bad for Vina before."

"Why didn't you claim her then?"

The breath I heaved out felt as heavy as the weight on my shoulders. "Thought it would cause issues with my kids because of her age. I already screwed up with Star, not having a better plan for her when she aged up and couldn't linger around the club without being claimed or being a part of things. I didn't want to drag a younger woman into the mix as the stepmother to my kids and also have it shoved in their faces that she used to be a club whore. At the time, I just pictured them comparing Kim to Vina and I don't know, it seemed impossible."

"You men and your hangups about the club girls." Scout rolled her eyes. "That was the biggest issue with Kip. He didn't want to claim a whore all his brothers might have been with, but then he wanted to be mad at me for having to do my job. For the record, I don't think either of your kids are the type to judge Davina based on her age and Star wouldn't care about her past as a club girl either. She's not judgy like that from what I've seen."

"Kip isn't either."

"The fact that we're not together and he had a kid with another woman begs to differ. He might not judge you for your decisions, but he certainly couldn't let my past go without shoving it in my face at every turn."

"Between you and me, I think he learned his lesson about that, sweetheart."

"Doesn't change everything that happened as a result of that lesson."

"You think you and my boy can ever work that shit out?" she shrugged and wouldn't look me in the eye. "If you can't handle that Knox is another woman's kid, then you need to make it clear as fuck to Kip that you'll never work. Don't give two shits how the two of you handle your business, as you're both grown-ass adults. I do, however, give a fuck when it comes to my grandson's well-being."

"I would never take my frustrations out on an innocent child," Scout countered.

"But can you *love* the child your man had with another woman?" She didn't answer right away and that led me to believe that she wasn't so sure. "Don't go there until you can answer that question without hesitating." I stood then. "Need to get back to my family, so get me that info. I want to know exactly where she's been and when she was there. Times and dates, Scout. Keep Kip and Bagger in the loop about staying vigilant and keeping the girls safe, too."

Scout nodded, but never lifted her eyes off her screen again. I let her have the moment, knowing how fucking hard it must be for her. The fact that she was helping me with an ex-girlfriend who might have gone off the deep end because I got another woman pregnant did not escape my notice. She was living her own similar nightmare out while watching my son be a father to a child he didn't make with her.

Thinking back, if either of my kids had turned out to be Kim's with another man, I'm not sure how I'd feel when put in that position. I loved my wife with everything I had, but the whole reason we got there was because we had a child binding us together. It forced us to try harder than we might have otherwise. I can see where the strain of a third party involved in the relationship might fuck up the dynamic and weaken the link. Scout was wise to take her time before she decided if she could handle it. I only hoped we didn't lose her as a result one day.

"Tripp!"

I turned to see June's cousin, Anna, jogging to catch up to me. "What do you need?"

"Um, well, I thought you should know that no one in the family has seen June or heard from her."

"That it?" I asked, still itching to get back to my girls.

"Well, her father is in critical care on the fourth floor and pretty bad off. He's not expected to make it, but she may use that as an excuse to get around inside the hospital."

"Thanks for letting me know. If you see her, you need to contact me immediately." I passed her a card with my number on it and she quickly slipped it into her pocket. Just as I started to walk away, she called me back again.

"Tripp?"

I turned, annoyed as shit that the once bold girl I knew back in high school suddenly seemed like she couldn't string a whole fucking sentence together without pissing her pants. "What?"

"It's just..." Anna paused and bit her lip as her eyes scanned the hallway we stood in. "June used to follow Kim around, too."

She had my full attention. "Something on your mind seems to be a bit more important than June simply following my wife around years ago. Spit it out, woman. I don't have time for a bunch of shit. Your cousin is already causing me enough headaches when I should be putting all my focus into my sick daughter."

She nodded her head and then gulped. "The day of the fire, we ran into Kim at the newspaper. She was there doing whatever it is that she did. I guess she took pictures for the paper sometime."

"I know what my wife did. Don't need a lesson in it, so get to the point."

"June was nasty to Kim and your wife turned it right back around on her. Embarrassed June and put her in her place where you were concerned. She flaunted how happy you guys were and how you never even thought about June at all."

"And?"

"My cousin was madder than a hornet comin' out of a kicked nest. She was angrier than I've ever seen her or any other human for that matter. Tripp, that was the same day as the fire at your house."

My stomach clenched tightly at what she insinuated. "You think she started that fire?"

Anna nodded. "June also went to the funeral. She watched you bury Kim and swore then that she'd get you back now that your wife was out of the way."

"And you didn't think to tell anyone this back then?"

"I didn't think she was crazy enough to kill her," Anna pleaded. "It wasn't until I saw that look in her eyes when she was asking me about your little girl that it really started to sink in that maybe that's exactly what she did."

"Jesus fucking Christ," I muttered before spinning around, so I could get back to Scout before she took off. When I got back to the cafeteria, Scout was still there, but so was my brother, Mack.

"I need you to remain calm when I tell Scout what I'm about to divulge. We're in public and I can't have you making a scene, I told my brother-in-law."

He pulled a chair out and took a seat while keeping his eyes locked with mine. "Fuck man. This better not be what I think it is." I tilted my head and really studied the man then. Had he always suspected June of setting the fire that killed his sister?

"I just ran into Anna," I explained. "June's cousin," I added when he didn't seem to know who Anna was.

His shoulders sagged and he turned his eyes down to the floor. "Fucking spit it all out already. It's not like she wasn't my number one suspect."

"It would have been nice to have known that all those years ago," I admitted. That was something we were going to have to discuss later, though. "Anna is worried because no one has heard from June. Her father is dying in this very hospital, giving her an excuse to hang around if she chooses to."

"Bet her father dying right at this very moment isn't all that coincidental," Mack muttered. He had a point, but I needed to get all the information to Scout so she could do some digging.

"Anna said that June used to follow Kim." Mack flinched as I said her name. It had been a good long while since either of us had spoken about her to one another. "She said that the day of the fire Kim ran into her and June at the paper. June tried to run her down verbally and Kim spouted some shit back and left. It was enough to rile June up enough that her cousin described her reaction as the angriest she had ever seen a human in her life."

"Fucking Kim. She never could just shut up and walk away."

"Nah, that shit isn't on her."

"No. It's fucking not."

"Not on me either, brother. I left that bitch behind in the past a long time ago."

"Yeah, except from what I hear you've been running around with that fucking cunt for months now behind everyone's back."

"Be glad to explain that situation to you, but I thought we were just rekindling a friendship, considering she's been married this whole time."

"So, you weren't dating her?"

I blew out a frustrated breath, because knowing what I did now, it killed to admit that I was. "It took that turn recently, though we hadn't been physical yet. Then Davina came into the picture with a daughter I didn't know was mine."

"If that cunt gets her hands on either of Kim's children, or Davina's for that matter, you and I will not be okay. You invited this trouble back into all our lives by not being able to leave the trash in the past."

"That's not true," Scout stated before I could agree with my brother.

"What do you mean?" I asked at the same time Mack demanded, "Explain."

"You told me to do a deep dive on her, and since she seemed to have a problem with your kids, I pulled the surveillance we had on Star. Bagger wasn't great about taking video proof of life for you, but his replacement was." She turned her laptop so we could both see what was there. "Trench obviously didn't realize there was a problem, since he probably had no clue who June was."

"Jesus," I hissed.

"Is that from five years ago?" Mack asked, his eyes just as wide in shock as my own had to be.

"It's a little over four years ago."

"Where was she when this was taken?"

"Wyoming, according to the file name," Scout answered.

"What the fuck was June doing in Wyoming?"

I pulled my phone out as Mack asked the question. "Baby girl, we need you to answer a question for us, and I need you to think really hard about your answer."

"Okay," Star responded hesitantly. I realized that I hadn't even greeted her when she picked up the phone, but it was too late for niceties.

"When you were in Wyoming, say four or five years ago, did you have any problems?"

"What kind of problems?"

"Unexplainable car troubles, getting sick out of the blue, someone knocking you around and making it seem like an accident."

"Holy shit," Star whisper yelled. "Do you think someone was targeting me?"

"Need you to answer the question, Star."

"Yeah, I had to put my car in the shop because the brakes weren't responsive. I nearly killed myself trying to stop when an elk stepped out on the road in front of me. Thankfully, I hadn't been going that fast. When I got the car stopped, I called for a tow."

"Your shadow didn't show himself to help out?" I asked.

"I sort of ditched Trench earlier in the day. In fact, the only reason he was able to follow me after was because of that stupid incident and having to put my car in the shop. I was headed out of town."

"Son of a bitch."

"Don't blame him. I sort of slipped something into his drink."

"You could have been killed, Star."

"And there would have been nothing he could do to save me if I'd been speeding out of town trying to get him off my ass as I drove."

"Fair point. Look, I gotta go deal with your uncle and Scout."

"Bagger is going to want to know what this was all about. He's been listening in beside me."

"Mack will fill him in when we're done here. Kip too. Love you, baby girl."

"Love you too, Dad."

I hung up and turned worried eyes on my brother. "Get a security detail on Knox, Kip, Star, Davina and Coral," then I turned to Scout. "And one for you too, darlin'."

"I don't need a security detail," she huffed.

"If June has been following my family around that long, then she knows you mean something to my boy and me."

"We should just arrange a lockdown," Mack suggested.

"I think you're right. Fuck's sake, we'd need to call other chapters in to get security for my family and they'd probably laugh their asses off when they found it was an ex high school girlfriend causing so much fuss." I shook my head, dismayed at the situation that we found ourselves in because of shit that happened when I was in high school.

"I don't get it. She may have been a little possessive at the end because she didn't want to be on the losing end, but we were already on the way to a split before shit went down with Kim. I never saw June as a psychopath capable of this shit."

"People change, man. Never liked the bitch because she had designs on changing you and never intended to stick around to be part of the club, but never saw this level of crazy from her either."

"I need to get up to my girls."

"Put the word out about lockdown for me, yeah?"

"I got you."

"Your old lady good?" I asked, remembering why he must have been at the hospital to begin with.

"Yeah, she's in radiology getting scan. Hoping everything's clear again, but they wanted to be sure."

"Hope like fuck my Coral can get that all clear before too long, as well."

"We're all praying for that, Tripp."

CHAPTER 18
DAVINA

I woke up to a full-body chill. It wasn't the kind that signified a person was cold. No, this was the type of chill that signaled there was a predator nearby, a fire, or some other catastrophe headed your way.

When my eyes drifted open, it was to see a nurse staring at my daughter with far too much interest. It seemed as though she was memorizing or cataloging her features as the woman slipped closer. Just as she reached for Coral's IV, she hesitated and turned to see me watching her.

I didn't even get to ask what she was doing before she startled and began to backpedal out of the room. It took me aback so much that I immediately reached for the nurse call button on the side of my daughter's crib.

"Can we help you?"

"There was just a nurse in here behaving oddly. Please, send someone in here. Not the nurse who was just here, though. I think she may have been trying to do something to my daughter."

Before I could get another word out an alarm blared over the hospital's announcement system. "Code Pink has been issued. Code Pink."

A nurse ran into the room and shut the door behind her immediately. I noticed a security officer stationed himself outside the door before she made her way over to me. "Someone from security will be here in a moment to take your statement. Can you describe the woman who was just in your room?"

"She had long brown hair, but it looked weird, like maybe it wasn't sitting right on her head. She was about average height for a woman and..." I was frustrated with myself because I couldn't remember much else. "I just woke up and saw her standing there looking at my daughter before she grabbed her IV line. When she noticed I was awake, she ran out of the room."

"Do you remember what she was wearing?"

"Basic blue scrubs. She had a mask on, but it wasn't pulled up on her face, it was just dangling around her neck."

"Okay, that's good." The woman pulled out her cell phone and started talking to someone on the other end of the line. She gave them the description I'd just shot off and then offered a tiny smile to me. "I know you're scared right now, but we have everyone in the hospital looking out for this woman. She was not a nurse, at least not the one assigned to your daughter – as that's me and I was standing at the nurse's station when you hit the call button. We have a code pink up throughout the hospital right now, it's basically like an in-house Amber Alert system. Even though your daughter wasn't taken, we are having security watch all the exits and the security cameras are all recording. Everyone will have to show ID and explain who they are here to see to access any floors beyond the first floor where emergency is."

"Okay. I still don't understand how some woman pretending to be a nurse could be in here. Why would anyone want to hurt my daughter?"

"I can explain that." I turned to see Tripp coming through the doorway with the security guard following behind him.

"Sir, you can't go in without showing your ID."

"It's okay, he's her father," I called out. The security guard didn't seem happy to be dismissed but still walked back out to stand guard in the hallway once more.

"What happened?"

The nurse and I filled Tripp in on what I woke up to and what the hospital was doing to try to locate the woman. Tripp wasted no time in getting his phone out and shooting off several messages via text. It wasn't until he was done that he asked the nurse to excuse us for a minute, so that we could have a conversation in private.

Tripp explained what he had learned from June's cousin and Scout, who had apparently had the woman under investigation on orders of her President. "So, you knew that she might come here?"

"I didn't think she could gain access to the floor anymore because the nurses caught her once before and chased her off when she attempted to follow us up here. We thought..."

I thought that we had it handled. Then Scout told me just a bit ago that they didn't have eyes on June and Anna told me that no one in her family had seen or spoken to her cousin for a couple days. Plus, June's father is suddenly on his death bed in this very hospital, and Mack thinks that isn't the coincidence it seems to be." Tripp scraped his hands through his hair and then yanked at his beard in frustration.

"I should have told you all this, but you have so much to worry about already with Coral. I didn't want to burden you with a problem that I brought into the mix."

My anger deflated immediately as I moved closer so that I could wrap my arms around Tripp.

We snuggled into one another for a few minutes before I turned my head up to look into his eyes. "Thank you for trying to give me peace, but I need to know when my daughter might be in danger. If that weird feeling hadn't woken me up, there's no telling what she might have done to my baby girl while I slept there unaware."

"Thank fuck for your feeling, whatever it was, waking you. Maybe it was Coral's angel."

"Maybe it was Kim, looking out for your daughter and making sure she didn't suffer the same fate."

Tripp choked back a sob at that. "Fuck, Vina." The words were whispered into my hair as he pulled me closer. "That's just what she'd do, too." He paused a minute and then cocked his head to the side. "Wait, why did you say that?"

"Say what?"

"The bit about Kim saving Coral from the same fate."

"I don't know. It was part of what woke me up. That feeling like, 'It's happening again.'"

Tripp pulled me into his arms and held me tightly as he explained the part he had left out earlier, that the new theory everyone had was that June was responsible for the fire that killed his wife.

"We'll get justice for her."

"We're not one hundred percent certain it was June," he admitted.

"After seeing that woman, and the way she looked at our daughter, I have no doubt about it. She was going to take our baby from us. Anyone who could do that to a child could easily do that to a woman she thought stole her life out from under her."

"Fuck," Tripp hissed again. "Kim called me the day she died and told me she had a weird feeling. She was worried about me; afraid I'd been harmed or something. All along, Kim was probably feeling what was coming for her that day. I should have gone home to her when she told me she felt like something was off. If I had, maybe I could have saved her."

"Tripp," I whispered and then leaned in and gently pulled his face down toward me. My hands rested on his bearded cheeks as I did so and I stroked over them gently, to ease the tension built in his shoulders. "You couldn't have known. I don't think anyone would ever expect for a person to behave the way your ex-girlfriend has. It's something straight out of Hollywood, not the reality most of us face."

"That's no excuse. My wife called me because she felt off and needed me to be there for her, to offer comfort and I stayed at work while she was murdered by someone that did it because of me."

"And none of that is your fault. Not even the part where you didn't go home. It wasn't something you normally would have done, right?" He shook his head slightly. "Kim never asked you to come home, did she?"

"No."

"Okay then. You didn't let her down because you couldn't have known. That is what makes hindsight a bitch. Please, stop torturing yourself about what might have been because it isn't possible to go back and change anything. You need to pull your focus back to the present. Your children are your number one priority."

"The club just went on lockdown today."

"Well, that's good. Star and Kip will be at the clubhouse, so you won't have to worry about them."

"I will be here with you and Coral. If, for some reason, I can't be here with you, one of my trusted brothers will be in this room and another outside that door until that bitch is caught."

There was a quick knock on the door then and the nurse opened up without waiting for us to tell her she could. "Sorry for the intrusion, but I wanted to give you an update. It seems that a nurse named Anna was the one whose badge was scanned into one of the med drawers. She isn't a nurse on this wing."

"It wasn't her," Tripp stated.

"I'm sorry, how do you know that?"

"I was talking to her about the same time that the fake nurse must have been in this room. Anna is the cousin of the woman whose photo has been passed around the floor. Her cousin June might have gained access to Anna's badge. Go find her. She works on the second floor, but her uncle is also a patient in the critical care unit on the fourth floor, so she might be there visiting. Find out if she's missing her badge."

"I will go let security know what you had to say. Could you tell me the exact time, and where in the hospital, you saw Anna? It might be helpful in tracing her steps forward and back to see where she might have come into contact with this other woman, or where her badge went missing."

"Sure, it was about twenty minutes before I showed up here and down in the hallway just off the cafeteria."

No sooner did the nurse leave the room than Tripp was on the phone. He called Scout and told her to work her magic and snag the hospital's security footage before anyone else could fuck with it. I had to admire my man. Shit. He wasn't really my man. Maybe in another reality. Tripp was just being nice to me because of the problems with our daughter and now June. He had vowed to take care of me, but I wasn't delusional enough to think it meant he wanted to be with me too. He had his reasons for not wanting more than one night, despite whatever crush he claimed to have on me before. Those reasons hadn't gone away.

CHAPTER 19
TRIPP

It didn't take long for Scout to gain access to the security footage and back it up on her own server. Then, she started pouring through the footage until she found where June entered my daughter's room and when she all but ran out of it about ten minutes later.

"Ten minutes." I growled into the phone. "That bitch had ten whole fucking minutes in this room with my daughter and my woman asleep and not knowing it. If she wasn't slow and sloppy for whatever reason, she could have taken them both out before anyone could do anything about it."

"They won't be left alone again," Scout asserted.

"Damn right they won't. If I'm not here, I want Breakneck or one of the other brothers not directly related to me by blood, marriage, or serious relationship."

"I will pass that along to Mack, so he can be the one to give the order to everyone."

"It's a direct order from their President, Scout. If anyone

hears it from you and doesn't fucking listen, I want to know about it."

"Sure thing, Prez."

We hung up after that. It seemed some of the club members had been giving Scout a hard time since she was the only female member. I wasn't going to have that shit on my watch as president. Mack would need to sort some shit and crack some skulls along with Breakneck if they were disrespecting one of the most productive and important members of our club. Scout did more with her computer and resources on any given day than most of the members combined contributed in a year. If they thought they were more important than her because they had a dick swinging between their legs, they had another thing coming.

"You okay?"

I turned just as Davina reached out and smoothed a finger across my furrowed brow, in an attempt to ease the tension.

"I'm so far from okay that I don't even know what it looks like anymore." The admission must have shocked her as much as it did me. "Sorry. Don't want to add any weight to your shoulders. I feel like every bit of this is my fault and I'm fucking out of my mind that no one has seen this bitch until today and she still managed to slip through our fingers again. She's not a fucking criminal mastermind. She's a spoiled ass rich cunt who is having a fucking more than two-decade long tantrum because she didn't get what she wanted."

"Well," Davina huffed in a teasing tone. "If any man was worth a two-decade long tantrum, it is definitely you."

"Fuck, woman," I growled as I pulled her, so our bodies were flush. "Are you okay?"

"I'm freaked out, but trying to deal because our girl can feel it when we're tense and afraid. I don't want her to think that has anything to do with her."

"You're right. From now on, June's bullshit doesn't cross the threshold of that door. Anything that needs to be discussed will happen out there." I pointed toward the hallway beyond where an armed security guard stood vigil.

AFTER SPENDING the night on the most uncomfortable hospital cot known to man, I was still elated to be there because my woman was wrapped up in my arms and my little girl had a decent night, for once.

Just as I was waking fully, a soft knock on the door, followed by my oldest daughter entering the room brought another smile to my face.

"What are you doing here?"

Star smiled down at me as her eyes drifted to the sleeping woman in my arms. "I like this for you," my daughter told me.

"This?" I asked, shocked that she seemed so happy about me cozied up to Vina.

"Yeah, this." She swirled a finger around indicating me, Vina, and our little girl. "It will be good for Coral to grow up in a happy home with both her parents the way Kip and I did.

You were always an amazing dad to us, and I have no doubt that Vina is just as good a mom as ours was. My little sister deserves to have the same experience, especially after everything she's been through. The two of you together could make that happen." Star grinned at me. "Well, the three of you together as a family."

"There's more than three of us in this family," I reminded my oldest daughter.

"I know that, Dad. Kip and I will be around too, and Knox." Star's bright smile lit up the room as she spoke. "Mom would approve," she said as she nodded her head toward Vina.

"Yeah? You think so?"

"I know so."

"How can you be so sure?"

"Because for the first time in years, I saw you at peace," she nodded toward Vina. "When you were wrapped around her, you were at peace. That is what Mom would have wanted for you to have. It's what I want for you too. So, if Vina brings you peace, you have our blessing."

"Thank you," I whispered huskily to my oldest daughter as my heart got stuck somewhere in my throat at the thought of her speaking for both herself and her mother's ghost. A feeling of complete contentment washed over me and bathed me in warmth, as if Kim was delivering her blessing along with my daughter's words.

"I was just stopping by to see if either of you needed anything. Bagger is waiting for me in the hall, trying to put his ear to the ground and see if someone says something that might be useful." When I told her that we were all good for now, Star leaned down and kissed my forehead and then went to do the same to her sister before she scooted right back out of the room just as quietly as she had come. My daughter didn't realize she'd already brought me the best gift possible that morning – her acceptance. What more could I possibly need?

CHAPTER 20
DAVINA

My eyes remained shut as Tripp's eldest daughter gave him her blessing for us to become a family. I wasn't sure if that was what he really wanted or if Star was reading too much into things. Lord knew I had done that once upon a time myself. It wasn't until after she was done checking in on my daughter, and left again, that I realized Tripp knew I'd been awake the whole time.

Tripp squeezed me tightly and then leaned in closer as he whispered to me. "I know you were awake and overheard that."

"I didn't want to intrude on your moment with Star."

"That's why you're perfect. You know that, right? You put everyone else before yourself." It felt like he was comparing me to other people, and maybe he was. Maybe he was comparing me to June or to his dead wife. Either way, I was just happy to come out on the positive end of things.

"Has there been any word about June?"

"No," He groaned as he got up off the little cot they gave

us to use. "Speaking of, I need to go check in with everyone at the clubhouse and see what's going on. I'm going to have someone here with you before I leave though." He added when he noticed my panicked expression.

"Thank you."

"Don't ever thank me for taking care of you and my daughter. I'm just realizing I didn't do a good enough job of protecting Kim when she was mine. You better believe I learned that lesson the hard way and won't allow history to repeat itself. You're mine now, Vina. That little girl right there, she's mine, too. We're a family and we'll make that official as soon as we can. While you sit with our daughter, I'm going to go make sure we track down the one person who is a threat to the two of you. I might not be able to do shit about the cancer, but I can try to do something about the dead woman walking."

It was on the tip of my tongue to tell Tripp I loved him. Instead, I swallowed that down and hugged him tightly. "Please, be safe. I worry about you too. She's been fixated on the females in your family because she thought they were weaker or easier to get to, but what happens when she turns that anger and bitterness on you?"

"How about I keep someone glued to my side, even though I'm not the least bit worried about myself. Will that make you feel better?"

"It really will. We need you to be safe. She needs you," I corrected.

"Well, that's good because I need both of you in my life to be happy. I fucked it up last time, and we will talk about that later when this other shit isn't hanging over our heads. But sweetheart, believe me when I say, it's good that Star gave her blessing, but you and me, that was going to happen no matter what. Having her blessing is icing on the cake because it means one more person in our family who won't let you down."

I was speechless. He remembered what I'd said that first time we were together about wanting a family who I could be there for and who would be there for me.

"Trench should be here in a minute," Tripp said as he glanced down at the text he'd just received on his phone. His lips turned up in a smile as he looked back up at me. "Mitzi and Dee are coming with him to keep you company."

"I haven't seen Dee since I was pregnant and Mitzi since before I left." The excitement over reacquainting myself with old friends meant that I let a little something slip that I probably shouldn't have.

"You saw Dee after you left the clubhouse?" Tripp asked.

I nodded in response. "Don't be mad at her. We ran into one another when she was out shopping and there was nothing to tell her about who the father was, so..."

"Don't worry, she's not in trouble," Tripp assured me.

"Good because withholding my pregnancy from the club was totally on me."

"Sweetheart, we all know why you did it and no one blames you. It sucks that the reason we found out was because of Coral's illness, but I'm fucking happier than hell it finally came out. I wouldn't want to miss a minute more of her life or the one I plan on spending with you by my side."

"Tripp," I whispered. He leaned in and placed a kiss on

the tip of my nose just as the door opened and Mitzi, Dee, and Trench came bounding inside the room.

"Keep it down. Baby girl is asleep, and she needs all the rest she can get right now," Tripp informed them before they could get too boisterous in their hellos. Once he was satisfied that they all took him seriously, he took off and left me to catch up with old friends.

CHAPTER 21
TRIPP

ONE MORE FUCKING week and no sign of the cunt whose agenda was to harm my family. Scout pulled some strings and had her investigator friend, the same one who helped find out all the shit about Kip's soon-to-be ex-wife, look into June.

"Dad!" Star called out as the door to the hospital room opened. I turned and put my finger up to my lips before she woke my girls. "Sorry," she whispered. "Rough night?"

"They started baby girl's new meds last night and they didn't agree with her," I admitted quietly. It was fucking awful to watch her get so sick and know that there was nothing anyone could do. The only thing that made Coral feel even a little bit better was to be in her mother's arms. She didn't want a damn thing to do with me, and I guess I couldn't blame her. I'd been here a lot, but my daughter slept most of her days away. That in itself was worrisome because it felt like she was sleeping more, not less. I wasn't sure how I would handle it if she couldn't survive this fight, but there was no doubt in my mind that it would absolutely destroy my woman.

"You here by yourself?" I asked Star, wondering what she was doing here with no one following her in the room.

She shook her head. "Bagger is here, too. He went to talk to the nurses. We thought that maybe if he put his pretty face to good use and flirted a bit with the nurses they would remember seeing a strange woman around who didn't belong."

I laughed quietly and pulled my oldest daughter in for a hug. "You cool with that tactic?"

She shrugged and smiled up at me. "It's for a good cause. Besides, I'm the one he's going home with, so no harm for him to be extra friendly and hopefully get us some useful information. This bitch stays underground much longer, and I'll set the whole town on fire to flush her out."

"Let's hope it doesn't come to that."

"We're also here because I think you and Davina need a break from the hospital, especially if you had a rough night. We're going to sit here with Coral."

I interrupted Star then. "Not sure that's a good idea. Last night, the only thing that settled Coral was being in her mom's arms."

"We'll make it work, and if she is truly inconsolable, I promise to call you both immediately." My daughter turned worried eyes toward the woman I planned to build a family with. "She looks run down, Dad. Vina needs some time away from here, too. She needs a good shower, some decent food, and rest that she can't get with nurses, doctors, and visitors popping in and out of the room at all hours."

"That is for damn sure," I mentioned. The stiff neck that caused my headache was partly because we had one tiny fucking cot to share and because I was constantly startled awake all night.

"You both need some rest."

"Yeah, you look like shit," Bagger agreed as he walked through the door.

"Anything?" Star asked as she popped up on her toes to receive a kiss from her man.

"Nada. The bitch either hasn't been here or has found better disguises."

"Well, that sucks. I was hoping she'd be hiding in a broom closet or something."

Bagger and I both laughed at my daughter as she pouted about not being able to find my elusive ex as easy as opening the janitor's closet.

"Hey, what's everyone doing?" Vina asked as she walked up behind me.

"We came to give you a few hours off," my daughter stated.

"The whole night, if you're willing. We'll be here with Coral every minute," Bagger added.

"We're worried about you not getting proper rest, food, and well... You both look like shit."

"Thanks," Vina said as she rubbed her neck in almost the same spot that also bothered me. I pulled her close and started to massage the kink out for her. Immediately the memory of her massaging the knots out of my back, that first time we were together, came to mind. I smiled down at her and kissed the crown of her head. I knew exactly what to do for my woman, if I could get her to leave the hospital with me. I was going to return the favor for her.

When I finally convinced Vina that our daughter was in good hands and that we both needed this break, I took her to the truck I'd brought to the hospital.

"No bike?" she asked as I helped her in because the damn thing was lifted too high. Unfortunately, it was the only vehicle available that didn't pose a huge security risk. It was also one that June had never seen me drive, to my knowledge. That was important because I didn't have the manpower to have a babysitter sit on the truck to make sure it wasn't tampered with.

"No. Figured the truck would be safer since we don't have eyes on the bitch yet."

"I suppose you're right about that. I wish she would just choke on a fucking dick."

I sputtered out a laugh as I threw a glance her way. "Don't you think that's what she's been gagging to do?"

Vina rolled her eyes at me. "Obviously, she shouldn't choke on *your* dick. That would be too kind to her. She should choke on a nasty, infected, puss-filled-"

I cut her off there. "Yeah, we don't need to be that descriptive. I get the picture."

"I guess I could keep it to myself, if you're sure you don't want all the details of the revenge dick I picture that bitch choking on?" Vina teased as we pulled out of the hospital and headed toward the clubhouse. "Where are we going anyway? It feels like an age since I've been to my apartment."

"Speaking of that," I said as I reached over and grabbed her hand for reassurance. "We should get you guys packed up and have your stuff brought to the clubhouse for now. The apartment isn't safe. Besides, when we bring our baby girl home, I want it to be somewhere we can all be together. I'll have a house built for us, but it will take some time."

"A house built," she parroted. "For us?" It was a question, and at the same time it felt almost like hearing a lost little girl ask if she really got to wake up to Christmas presents waiting for her.

"Yeah, sweetheart, for us. You, me, and our daughter. Want us together from here on out."

"Do you really think June knows where I live or that she would show up there?"

I hated that she felt the need to change the subject, but I let it go knowing that my woman had a hard time accepting that she was mine now. That was something we would work through before we went back to the hospital. I wanted Vina to know in no uncertain terms that she was mine. The claim had already been made within the club, and I was just waiting on her to catch up. Normally, I would have gone a pushier route with her, but with our daughter in the hospital, she was under enough strain already.

"We have someone watching your apartment as well as the office where you worked, just in case. Figured June might try to pretend she needs some legal help to get an in to get closer."

Vina shivered visibly before she spoke. "I honestly can't understand this level of crazy. Was she always like this? You used to date her in high school. Were there no red flags back then that she was completely off her rocker?"

I shook my head. "Not back then. At least, not the way

you mean. There were probably red flags that we weren't a good match and I ignored them for far too long before Kim came around. She did not take things well after Kim got pregnant, but that was another story altogether. It felt like she was justified in her anger back then and the only really crazy thing she ever attempted was to get me to go home with her and leave the girl I got pregnant to fend for herself."

"That was red flag enough. Any woman who would willingly ask you to leave your responsibilities, especially a child, behind to tend to her selfishness clearly has problems."

I chuckled at that because my woman wasn't wrong. "We weren't right for one another. The relationship we had back then, it was kids in high school hooking up and in her case, defying her parents and rebelling as much as she was able. When push came to shove and it was time for me to graduate and start working more for the club, she couldn't handle the club business aspects, me living in a clubhouse where club girls were within easy reach, and..." I stopped there because Vina flinched.

"There's nothing wrong with club girls. June's issue was that she didn't think I would be faithful to her if fresh pussy was on tap outside my bedroom door 24-7."

"I hate to break it to you, Tripp, but most women would feel that way."

"Yeah, I suppose they would. You know who didn't?"

"Who?"

"Kim. She never had issues with the girls at the club because even though we technically got together because I cheated on my then girlfriend, she didn't think I'd ever step out on her."

"Did you?" she asked.

"Never. She was right. June and I were pretty much broken up before she left for Europe that summer. Even if we hadn't had the official talk yet. I had plans to tell her we were done when she got back. Not that it's an excuse. It's just how things happened back then when we were young and a whole lot more carefree and less careful than I should have been."

"I get it. Things seem complicated and fleeting when you're that age. I'm glad you had Kim in your life and knew happiness with her. It sounds like you were a great match."

I nodded. "We were and yet we also had to work to stay that way. Relationships are harder than people let on. There are times when you forget how important the other person is and that you need to make time for them. You take things for granted and before you know it, you're sitting at a distance wondering how things changed so much and why you're not close anymore."

"That happened with you and Kim?"

The shocked tone in her voice lets me know that the history of Kim and I that got shared around the club was a version that painted everything as perfect all the time. "Marriage is work. When we realized we were slipping away from one another because of my duties to the club and hers as a mom, it took a while for either of us to really put it together that we needed to make one another a priority again or end up another sad statistic."

"It's good that you were able to do that."

"Yeah, and that's why we're going to be honest with one another about what we want and how we're feeling. Vina, if you need a break, you need to tell me. I was trying to stay at the hospital to be strong for you and our daughter, but it never really occurred to me until Star pushed for us to get some time away today that the thing you needed most was to get away."

Vina sighed and then bowed her head, as if she was ashamed of herself. "I wanted to be there and be strong for Coral, too. It feels like I'm betraying her every time I have to leave."

"You're not, though. The only betrayal would be if you wore yourself down so much that you were no longer able to be there for her. I need you to start taking breaks every day. We'll work out a rotation for who is there with Coral and it will never be someone you don't approve of."

"You're right. Neither of us can keep going like this without taking breaks."

"I don't mean to keep bringing up my former wife, but it was something Kim and I figured out later than we should have. We have to prioritize ourselves, each other, and the kids as if they're all separate things that need equal attention because they are. In our case, we also have to add in the club and your job, assuming you want to continue to work."

"I love my job. I love Gloria and Mr. Avery too. They've been there from the very beginning with Coral and me. Mr. Avery was the one who took me to the hospital when I went into labor. I can't... I couldn't leave him in the lurch. It's bad enough that I've had to take so much time off to be with Coral and then the lockdown because of June. I'm surprised he hasn't replaced me yet. I make a lousy paralegal when I'm not there to do my job."

"I think Mr. and Mrs. Avery are doing just fine while they wait on you to come back."

"How do you know that?"

"I talked to them. Someone had to explain why they had strange people camped out near their office and home. Mr. Avery called the cops a couple times. He thought it was someone he was suing on your behalf trying to intimidate him."

"Oh no! My mind has been so full of getting Coral well that I didn't even think of that. And Gloria never mentioned anything when she came to visit either."

"She probably didn't want to add to your worry. I took care of it and they're both on the lookout for June now, so that's an extra set of eyes."

"It's still hard to believe that you have an ex that is this..."

"Crazy?" I finished for her.

"Psycho," she filled in at the same time.

"It makes me want to kick my own ass for even entertaining a friendship with the woman, let alone the possibility of anything else."

Vina patted the hand I had settled on her thigh. "She was different to your face. It's what psychos do. They charm, they lie, they do whatever it takes to reach the goal they want. They eliminate the people who hinder that or find ways to sweeten up the ones who have to help with their efforts."

"You sound like you know from personal experience."

Vina sighed and turned to look at me. "I had a shitty upbringing and if it's all the same to you, I'd rather not spend our one night away talking about my miserable existence prior to me getting involved with the Savage Vipers."

"Fair enough, but eventually, we will talk about it."

"I imagine there will be plenty of time to discuss both of our families in depth."

She had me there, since I'd never willingly told anyone else about my upbringing, mom, or my father and brother – both of whom were formerly members of the club. They were probably both rolling over in their graves knowing that I was the president of the Savage Vipers MC. Then again, they had both been locked up before I ever even started prospecting for the club.

When we got to the clubhouse, Vina looked a little shell-shocked to be there again.

"It's all good, I promise."

She shook her head, but I could see a sheen of tears in her eyes. "Sorry," I know it's ridiculous, but I never thought I'd be back here again."

"If it bothers you, we can go somewhere else. I'm fairly certain the apartment Mack and Viv rent out is free again."

"No, we don't have to go anywhere. Being at the club-house isn't a bad thing, Tripp. I just never thought... I always dreamed of making this place my home, you know?"

"You did?"

She looked up at me with a sheepish grin on her face. "You weren't the only one who had dreams of what it would be like if only that other person noticed you and took you seriously."

"I always noticed you."

"Maybe, but you didn't take me seriously because of my position as a club girl."

"It wasn't just that."

"Then what?"

"Your age, sweetheart. You're closer to my kids' ages than mine."

"We're only 14 years apart, Tripp."

"Yeah, and you're only what? Five years older than my son?"

"Whatever. I assume you realize that it doesn't matter now?" She phrased it as a question as if it was important for me to answer.

"You're right. It isn't something that matters now. It shouldn't have mattered then, but I panicked."

Davina laughed. "I think we're all entitled to a little panic from time-to-time. Lord knows, I panicked when I hauled ass out of the club after that test came up positive."

"Prez!" Someone called out. When I looked around and couldn't pinpoint who it was, I decided to nip shit in the bud.

"Listen up!" I yelled. Everyone got quiet and turned their attention to me. "As you can see, I have Davina with me. In case any of you missed the fucking memo, she is my woman. We've had a little bit more to worry about beyond getting her a property patch and ink, so it hasn't happened yet, but you will all treat her as if it already did." A few catcalls and hoots and hollers went up, but I held my hand up to silence that shit too.

"When the time is right, we'll celebrate our union. For now, we're both exhausted and in desperate need of some sleep. Aside from the food I'm about to order, I don't want to be disturbed for anything unless someone is coming to tell me they found the woman we've been looking for."

I didn't wait for responses from anyone and continued through the clubhouse and back down the hall to my room.

"You just claimed me in front of your club," Davina said, sounding as though she was in shock.

"Already claimed you with my club before. This is just the first time you heard it. Not the first time I told you that you were mine, though."

Once I had the door shut and locked, I looked at Davina and smiled. "Why don't you get undressed and lay face down on that bed?"

"I might fall asleep on you if I do that."

"That's okay, sweetheart. It's time for me to pamper you for a change." I moved to toss my cut on the desk before I grabbed my phone out of my pocket and started scrolling for the diner that was closest to us. "Gonna order some food for us. You in the mood for anything specific?"

Vina chuckled. "Anything that doesn't come out of a vending machine or hospital cafeteria will be welcome. I would almost consent to eating Brussel sprouts if someone cooked them up for me." I laughed along with her because I couldn't stand the tiny little cabbage wanna-bes either.

"They said forty-five minutes, so that's how long you get with me trying to loosen these muscles. Then I'm going to feed you, and then we're going to take a nap."

She looked a little disappointed as she asked, "Is that all?"

"Nope, you didn't let me finish. At some point, I'm going to wake you up from that nap and make love to you. Then we'll take another nap, and eventually I'm going to wake up again and want to fuck you into next week. I hope you're ready, sweetheart."

"Oh God!" she mumbled. "So ready, Tripp. So damn ready for you."

After her massage and some good southern cooking from the diner, we both fell asleep.

When I woke, it was to my beautiful woman staring into my eyes. "I thought you'd never wake up."

"You could have coaxed me awake easily enough." I reached out and moved her hand onto my already hardening cock.

"I wasn't sure how much nap time old men needed," she teased as her hand flew up and down, spreading my precum all over my head and shaft.

"Is that so?" I asked before I flipped her over onto her hands and knees. "Are you wet for me, sweetheart?"

She nodded her head, and thank fuck for that, because I was like a starved man and the only thing that could possibly quench my appetite was her. I sank my cock deep into her pussy and groaned in relief that it was finally back where it belonged.

"Make it hurt so good, Tripp," Vina demanded. "Want to feel you later when I can't have you inside me."

"You must have forgotten that you can have me whenever you want me now, Vina. No need to miss my cock inside you."

She moaned loud and low as I thrust harder into her while keeping a firm grip on her hips. Every time I pushed forward, I pulled her back to meet me. My thighs slapped against hers in a wickedly fast cadence as my beautiful woman grew slicker between her legs. She drenched me in the best way. "Are you a squirter, sweetheart?"

"No." Her answer was pushed out abruptly with my last thrust. "Yes," she whimpered on the next thrust as we both felt her gush. "May... Be..." She moaned as her body became a boneless mess in my hands.

"Stay with me, sweetheart. We aren't nearly done yet." I circled my hips as I thrust in that time and then tipped Vina's hips just the slightest bit again. When I hit her spot that time, she went absolutely nuts, wailing and crying out for more.

"God! Yes, Tripp. Fuck me just like that."

"Like this?" I asked as I dragged my cock across the sensitive patch inside of her again only to slam home once more.

"Yes, Yes, don't stop."

"Never," I answered as I continued to rock into her with a damn near brutal force. She would be wearing my finger marks on her hips for a couple days as it was, but her pussy had also taken a pounding already and she continued to beg for more.

"Tripp," she whined my name until it was nothing but an unintelligible moan. Her pussy gushed on me once more to the point where I knew the mattress was most likely ruined for the night.

"Holy fuck, sweetheart. That's the hottest fucking thing I've ever seen."

"Mmmm." I was certain that was the only thing she was capable of saying as I rode her body down into the bed and gave a few last thrusts that brought my orgasm out and had me flooding her pussy with a hot load of my come.

A knock on the door startled us both out of our post-orgasm haze.

"Who the fuck is it?"

"Grady, Prez. Wouldn't have bothered you and the misses unless it was important."

"Is it Coral?"

"No, it's the bitch. She's been sighted."

"Be there in five," I announced as I crawled off Davina and moved to grab us both a towel out of the bathroom.

"Can I come too?"

"You want to hear the update about June?"

"Of course. She's been terrorizing my – our – family. I need to know where she is and if someone is able to snatch her up."

"Our family. Don't forget that shit," I stated as I leaned in and took her mouth in a punishing kiss. "You can come with me. You're right. She isn't just a club problem, and you deserve to know what's going on. Get dressed and you can hobble your way to the office with me."

"Hobble my way..." Vina rolled her eyes as she mimicked me, and my fucking heart felt like it might explode and melt inside my chest all at once. I was gone for the woman, and her teasing nature even if she still didn't fully realize it.

CHAPTER 22

DAVINA

ONCE I WAS DRESSED, Tripp escorted me to his office, just down the hall from his bedroom. "You sure you want to be here for this?"

"Positive. I need to know what she's been up to and how close we are to catching her."

As soon as we entered the office, Tripp's former brother-in-law stood there and eyed me curiously. "Vina," he stated. It wasn't done coldly, but there was no warmth in his greeting either. I guess I couldn't blame him since Tripp had once been married to his sister and I was the new woman. According to Mitzi and Dee, when they came to see me, some of the club girls were circulating a rumor that I'd gotten pregnant on purpose and only left before telling anyone because I got scared about what the men might do to me. Mack's less than inviting greeting made me wonder if he thought the same was true.

"Not sure you want her in here for this, brother."

"She wants to be here for updates on June, and considering she and Coral are both in that bitch's sights, I thought it was prudent that she hear this shit firsthand."

Mack sighed. "You might regret that in just a few minutes."

"Grady said she'd been found."

"Nah, Grady said she's been sighted. Scout has been getting help from some biker chicks upstate in the mountains. Turns out their little hacker has an in with law enforcement databases that Scout sometimes has a problem with. Keys, the biker chick up there, put feelers out and added a few names to her search parameters. One of them got a hit this morning. There was also a credit card purchase by one June Hargrove Whitaker not fifteen miles from where Barry Whitaker was found butchered in his brand-new condo."

"Barry is dead?" Tripp asked, sounding shocked by that news.

"He and his bedmate were both hacked to death. Barry was stabbed 72 times while the woman with him had her throat slit. According to the file Keys pulled and sent to Scout, the woman died first. The assailant apparently didn't have beef with her, except that she was in the wrong condo at the wrong time. Barry-boy wasn't so lucky. His death was prolonged. He was tied to the bed, and she sliced and diced him with minimal cuts at first. Then she started going deeper and hitting sensitive areas along the way too."

"What did they consider sensitive areas?" I asked.

Mack turned his eyes to me and spilled the details I

should have never asked for. "Barry's cock was chopped off and stuffed up his ass. His balls were also severed from his body and stuffed in his mouth. A whole fuck of a lot of rage went into his death."

"Jesus fucking Christ." Tripp muttered. "Fuck, sweetheart, I'm sorry I brought you in here now. You didn't need to hear any of that." Tripp pulled me into his body and cocooned me in his arms as Mack spoke.

"Sorry about the graphic details, but she wanted to know, and she asked for more."

"There's a way to deliver that shit," Tripp scolded him.

"No," I shook my head where it rested on his chest. "Mack is right. I wanted to know and now I do. That woman cannot get anywhere near my daughter. Who is with Coral right now?"

"She's fine," Mack answered. "Star, Bagger, and Kip are all there. Breakneck would be, but he has his own shit going down with Knox's very pissed off nanny. My wife has Knox right now, since he can't be at the hospital, and she's here hunkered down since we're spread too thin on security details to keep them at everyone's private residences."

"So, the only thing we have on June is that her credit card was used not far from where Barry was found?" Tripp asked.

"Yep. Barry was found at his condo in Savannah and June's card was used for gas at a station near Pembroke."

"We don't have eyes on her?"

"Not currently. Gas station didn't have cameras, so that was a bust, but between Scout and her buddy, they're trying to backtrack her possible steps to see if they can find her on any other cameras, so we can get a fix on what kind of vehicle she's driving."

"Thanks, Mack. Keep me posted. I'm going to get another quick nap with Vina before we head back to the hospital."

"Give that sweet girl a kiss for me when you get there." Mack stated, but then he looked my way and offered up a wink to let me know he didn't intend to be mean to me. At least, that was how I took it.

I nodded and Tripp said, "Will do."

We were back in the bedroom before anyone spoke again. "Tripp, it sounds like she's escalating in a big way, if June did this."

"I have no doubt June did this. My only question is why she did that to Barry. He gave her the divorce she wanted."

"Yeah, but maybe he didn't do it soon enough, since you know... You said that you saw her with him and froze her out for a few months, but during that time, you were with me, and I got pregnant. Maybe she blamed him for that happening."

"Could be. Could also be that she found out one of his mistresses was her cousin, Anna."

"Has anyone bothered to check on Anna?"

"No, I'll get a team together and go check her place, but she isn't my priority. We'll do that after."

"After?" I asked.

"Yeah, sweetheart. After I have you again and we get some shut eye. Once I deliver you back to the hospital – with security – I'll go with some of the guys to check on Anna."

"Okay. I hate that you have to go there, though. What if Anna's place turns into a trap?"

"Never been there before, so I don't see how that could be possible."

Tripp held up his end of the deal and thoroughly ravished me before we got our nap in, and he took me back to the hospital.

ABOUT TWENTY MINUTES after Tripp left the hospital to go check on Anna, Doctor Jenkins came in to see me.

"I hear you've had quite the change in circumstances, young lady." His warm smile let me know that he was not judging those changes. The kind man patted my hand and then gave it a little squeeze before he let go. "It's a good thing to have more family at your back as you and your daughter go through this challenging process. I'm glad you're back today because I wanted to talk to you about Coral's latest results."

He must have seen the panic in my eyes because Dr. Jenkins quickly shuffled me over to a chair and had me sit. Then, he took the one that was next to me and slid it around so that we were face-to-face as he gave me the results.

"Breathe, I promise it isn't bad. You were worried because Coral has been sleeping a lot more, but I'm here to tell you that the sleep has been restorative. I think you'll start seeing a turnaround in your little one's energy levels from here on out. Her labs were just this side of glorious," Dr.

Jenkins crowed, and I could see a little mistiness in his eyes as he teared up.

"Wait," I took a moment to get my breath. "You're telling me that she's doing better?"

"I'm telling you that her labs looked amazing. We're not totally in the clear yet, but the latest round of meds seem to be doing the job."

"So, what about the bone marrow thing?"

"With any luck, she will continue to respond well to the regimen she's on now and a transplant won't be necessary."

"Okay, so if she goes into remission, what are the odds that it comes back?"

"We'll have to bridge that gap when we get to it. The good news about not needing a bone marrow transplant now is that it will remain an option in the future. Not that she'll need it, but with this type of cancer, there really are no guarantees. The fact that she got this so young is testament to that. She's the youngest case on file in this country. Let's hope she continues to be a record-breaker, but in a positive way."

"Thank you so much for coming to tell me. I wish Tripp had been here, but he had business to attend to."

"Understandable. If Coral's father needs to contact me, he can reach me here," Dr. Jenkins held out his card for me to take.

"I can't thank you enough for taking such good care of my daughter and being so kind to us."

The doctor shook his head and patted my hand once more. "You and Coral had a rough start of things. It's the least I can do to mitigate the harm done in the early stages when you were vigilant in trying to obtain care for your daughter while this hospital's staff denied you doing what was best for her. You both deserved better. I'm just happy I was there to intercede for you and get your daughter on the path to healing."

CHAPTER 23
TRIPP

I CURLED up on the cot behind my woman. "Hey, did you find Anna?" Vina asked in a sleepy voice.

"No, and there was no answer at her place. If Scout can't get a lock on her tonight, we're going to have to break in and check things out. Something feels off about her disappearing into thin air, but then again, none of her family has raised an alarm that she is missing either. The hospital said she's taking a leave of absence after her cousin misused her badge. That leave of absence wasn't exactly Anna's choice. It's possible that she's running from the whole situation."

"It's also possible that her cray-cray cousin murdered her and stuffed her body in a freezer somewhere."

"Yeah, after seeing what was done to Barry, I'd say anything is possible at this point."

"Do you think she's really the one who killed Kim?"

"I don't want to bring my deceased wife, or my psycho ex into a bed we're sharing, sweetheart. Even if that bed is just a shitty hospital cot."

Davina got up and walked over to one of the chairs and took a seat then patted the one next to her. I did one better and picked her up and sat her back down in my lap. She snuggled in immediately.

"Now, tell me about Kim. I want to hear about the woman who had your heart first because she's an important part of your life, especially since you have Kip, Star, and Knoxville to think about. They need to know that her memory won't be buried and forgotten just because I'm in the picture with Coral. And I need you to understand that I'm not threatened by your first love.

"I don't consider June to be that. She was your first infatuation, lust at best, but never love because she tainted it." I hugged her closer as she said that last bit because it was honestly how I felt as well.

"No woman you ever date should be intimidated by the woman you loved and lost. She is your past, but she will always be important and relevant. I don't ever want you to think otherwise."

"There won't be any other women I date. You're it, Vina. Kim is probably smiling down at how perfect you are right now." I laughed as I admitted it. "Of course, she's probably also cracking cradle robbing jokes at my expense."

Vina laughed and the sound healed something inside me I didn't know needed to be mended. "Would she really do that?"

"Yeah, you bet your ass she would. Kim was one-of-a-kind."

I told Vina about how Kim and I started and the rocky beginning we had, then I told her about how we fell in love along the way and had a marriage most people would be envious of.

"That's a lot to live up to," she admitted.

"Nope. There's nothing to live up to. That was my story with Kim. My story with you is just starting. While it might have started out a little rough, too, we'll find our own pace and make our own happy along the way. What we have shouldn't be compared. Kim is my past, another life I lived before this one. You're my future, and we make of that what we're both comfortable with.

"I know you think I need to keep Kim front and center, but she hasn't held that spot in my life for many years. I appreciate you being willing to make room for her beside us, but that's no longer her place. There's just you and me here. Her memory can exist in my heart and with my kids and grandson. I'm happy as hell that it won't bother you if we discuss her, but I want you to know that she's not here. She's not going to come between us because I don't want that, and Kim wouldn't want it that way either. She would want us to have a fresh start with one another without another woman coming between us, even the ghost of another woman."

"If only there wasn't an evil other woman in the mix, too." Vina lamented. "What advice would Kim give me about dealing with June?"

"She'd tell you to have no mercy, but if I get my way, you will never need to follow that advice. I plan to make sure June isn't a concern for long. As soon as we find her, she'll be dealt with. Mack wants his pound of flesh just as much as I do."

"Oh God!" Vina's eyes went wide. "What will he think of

me? I was a little worried the other day because he wasn't exactly friendly."

I grinned at her. "Mack already gave his blessing, too. His abrupt nature and coldness wasn't for you, it was for me because he didn't like that he would have to give you the gory details of what happened to Barry. That was my fuckup because I wasn't thinking it could be something that heinous, or I would have sheltered you from it."

"I'm glad you didn't. It helps to know what we're really up against. I'm kind of shocked that Mack gave his blessing though. I didn't think anyone would want to see you with a club whore."

"You're not a club whore. You're a mother, a paralegal, a beautiful, intelligent, go-getter. You're the woman who took care of my baby girl on your own and you did an amazing job so far, sweetheart. You don't have to do it alone anymore. You're my old lady, and one day soon, you will also be my wife. What you did in the past, that's your past. No one cares. They only care that we're happy moving forward."

I wiped away her tears as she cried in disbelief and then filled me in on her life before the club. It made me fall in love with her ability to persevere just a little bit more. Vina had been through a lot, and she had never given up. Instead, she kept remaking herself into a better version with each obstacle thrown in her path.

"Oh, by the way, I have something for you," Vina said as she got up off my lap and walked over to where her bag rested against the little side table in the room. She pulled out what looked like a business card and brought it over to me.

"Here," she said and then bit into her bottom lip to stop the smile from spreading across her face.

"What's this?" I asked as the card turned over in my hand and I read the name on it. "Dr. Jenkins? As in our daughter's oncologist?" Vina nodded. "What exactly is this for?"

"In case you have any questions."

"About?"

"About the fact that our daughter's labs came back and..." Vina burst into tears. I stood immediately and grabbed a hold of her.

"Fuck, baby, I'm going to need you to spit it out because you have me in pieces seeing you like this. How much time do we have?"

"Hopefully, all the time in the world. She's on the mend, Tripp. Our baby girl is doing so much better. That's why she's been sleeping so much. She's been healing her little body. Dr. Jenkins thinks we'll be talking remission soon without the need for the bone marrow transplant."

"Are you kidding me?"

"Nope, he came by to talk to me not long after you took off."

"Shit, I wish I had been here for that."

"That's why he gave me his card for you. If you need to ask him questions, you can call or find out when he'll be doing rounds again, so that you can be here."

"Sweetheart?"

"Yeah, Tripp?"

"How about next time you lead with the amazing news and then we can slip into all the other stuff?"

Her giggle was music to my ears. I held onto Davina and

we both shed a few happy fucking tears. Tears of joy, relief, fuck... Just tears to wash away the weeks and months of worry. The only thing standing in the way of our happiness as a family now was my ex-fucking-girlfriend. When I got my hands on her, I would make sure she suffered every bit as much as her victims did. Fuck Barry Whitaker. I didn't give a rat's ass about the man, but what she put my wife through, my new old lady, our daughter, my other children, and my whole fucking club... She'd pay for all of it.

HOURS after I got to spend some quality time with my wide-awake baby girl and my woman, they were both finally fast asleep and resting. I was still up because that feeling in my gut was heavy. When it got to the point that it was all I could think about, I decided to stay up and on guard. Something was coming for us, and I didn't know what or when, but this feeling was something to be trusted.

My cell phone buzzed, as if it was a harbinger of doom.

> Scout: Need you at the clubhouse. Keys rode down yesterday, and we worked on tracking backward until we found the bitch.

> Tripp: You can't tell me what you found over the phone?

Scout: Mack requested that you be here for this. Bagger and Star are on their way to take your place.

Tripp: Anyone else around who you can send with them? I have a gut feeling that hasn't settled in the last hour or so.

Scout: Sorry, no. Everyone else is either on a run, here where they're needed, or on their way to look over your girls. We're pretty thin on resources right now.

Tripp: Headed out as soon as Bag and Star are here.

By the time I got to the clubhouse, I was already over the trip. My head hurt, my gut was telling me something bad was about to go down, and there was nothing I wanted more than to get back to my girls. I would settle for ending June's life as a consolation prize, but something told me that wouldn't be why they dragged me down to the clubhouse.

"Whatever you have better be worth the trip I just took," I called out the minute I walked into the clubhouse. Then I noticed a strange, red-headed woman who stood there smirking while she assessed me. "Who the fuck are you?"

"I'm the bitch who uncovered some helpful shit about your stalker," she countered.

Her cut identified her as a member of the all-female motorcycle club located in the northern part of the state. S.H.E. MC had become notorious years ago when they took out a sex trafficking ring that was snatching Georgia girls and selling them all over the world. They had my respect for how they handled the whole thing, especially since there were other MCs directly in the trafficking pipeline who had done nothing to stop it.

"Sara Keys, Security Officer for S.H.E. MC." The woman offered her hand to me and once we shook, I nodded my head in respect.

"Tripp Martin, President of the Savage Vipers, Danville, Georgia Chapter."

"Well, Tripp Martin, I don't want to keep you away from your family too long, so let's get to it." I followed her back to one of our meeting rooms we used when we had too many people to situate comfortably in my office but needed more privacy than the common room offered. The room we used as Church was off limits to anyone outside the club, no exceptions.

"Keys and I worked our way back from that gas station. We were able to get her on camera not too far from the condo where her ex-husband was found," Scout mentioned as she worked the keys on her laptop for a few minutes before an image was projected onto the screen on the opposite wall from where I was seated at the head of a conference table.

"Who the fuck is that?" I was looking at a large man with dark, slicked back hair and a gnarly scar that ran down the side of his face.

"That is Kenneth Winslow, Barry's brother-in-law.

Kenneth Winslow's real name was Anton Oslav." Keys told me.

"Anton Oslav? Why does that name sound familiar?"

"He was one of the bastards we were after a few years ago. He was part of the trafficking ring my MC took down. To be specific, he was the spoke in the wheel that took women to be dispersed throughout the Czech Republic and various countries surrounding them."

"What the fuck is June doing with that bastard?"

"We believe he is now working as a contract killer. In fact, he has been working as a contract killer for years now."

"When we catch June, if this fucker isn't with her, we need to interrogate until we find him."

I turned to my brother-in-law. "What aren't you saying, Mack?"

He released a deep breath before moving closer and taking the seat directly to my left. "My sister only died in that fire because she was incapacitated first."

"What the fuck?" I yelled. "Where did you get that information and fucking when?"

"My sister would have had to be knocked the fuck out before she allowed herself to burn up in a fire, especially when she was expecting the kids home soon." Mack stated. "I had the medical examiner do an autopsy. While everyone else believed her cause of death was fire related, I had my own suspicions."

"Why the fuck did you never share them with me?"

"You didn't need the distraction. You just lost your wife; the kids lost their mom. Your job was to be there for them and to not drown in the pain. It was my job to make sure we had all the facts in hand when the time was right."

"You always suspected June, didn't you? You mentioned that before."

"Fucking right I did, and it turns out I was correct." Mack wasn't being a smug ass about it. He was simply stating facts. "Couldn't prove that shit, but this makes sense. No way June did it on her own and got away with that shit. She's too fucking messy, as she proved with the Barry debacle."

"You think this same fucker helped June kill Kim?"

"She suffered blunt force trauma to the side of her head before she was burned in that fired. The blow killed her, the fire only covered up the evidence, brother."

"Part of me thinks that was better. I always thought she suffered, trapped in that house without a way to get out."

Mack nodded. "Thought the same until the autopsy came back. She wasn't trapped when that fire was set, she was killed just before." He jabbed a finger toward the man on the screen with June. "That fucker was a part of it. I'd bet money on it."

"Son of a bitch."

"I can verify that claim," Keys stated.

"How the fuck can you verify shit that happened all those years ago?"

Keys leaned over Scout and hit a couple keys. The image on the screen changed and a picture of my daughter and her then best friend, Ash came onto the screen.

"What the fuck?" I asked.

"Anton Oslav – aka: Kenneth Winslow – was meant to take these two girls as payment for something. The dates on the picture coincide with the time he would have been hired to kill your wife."

"Motherfucker!" I yelled as I stood and paced the room. "You're telling me that my baby girl was in the sights of these fucking traffickers way back then? She was a fucking child."

Key's voice lowered and I could feel the empathy in it. "That's when they like to take them. It's easier to break children and bend them to your will than adults. There are also those who prefer to purchase younger slaves."

"Arrrrgggg!" I growled as I slammed chairs into the wall. "That fucking cunt sicced kid peddlers on my child? Killed my wife. I want her death to be slow, painful, and I want her to have to see pictures of all the beautiful fucking moments I shared with Kim. She needs to suffer in every way possible. Don't care what it takes, but she needs to be found yesterday."

CHAPTER 24
DAVINA

"Age is just a number at a certain point. You're both adults, and one thing I learned I my travels is that you can't help who you fall for, especially when your heart aches for that person. I would never deny either you or my father your chance at happiness. I certainly wouldn't take away the chance of my sister having a happy, intact family simply because I'm too selfish to get over something as trivial as an age difference."

I listened as Star gave me her opinion on my relationship with her father. It was comforting to know that she felt the way she did. I'd been surprised to find her in the hospital room when I woke up instead of Tripp, but she had quickly assured me that she and Bagger were there to look out for us while he was handling business.

"I grew up with two loving parents and was lucky for it. Coral deserves to grow up the same way. She'll be a little luckier though because she has me, Kip, and Knox in the mix, too. Maybe Scout, if my brother ever pulls his head out of his ass where she's concerned."

"I appreciate you being so nice to me about this, but if it is a problem, I'd rather know the truth."

Star shook her head. "I meant every word I said. Besides, I already saw how you react to cheaters when you thought I was the other woman at Bagger's house." We both laughed about that. "It feels like a good plan to have another woman around who won't tolerate that bullshit. These guys have their loyalty to one another, but we need our own crew that has one another's back. Not that I think my dad would ever step out on you. He's far too enamored to even think of anyone else, truth be told."

"It seems like Bagger feels the same about you," I reminded her.

"I suppose so. We're still building trust after a bumpy start."

"Speaking of, where is Bagger?"

"He just went down to get our food really quick. We tried to have something delivered, so you wouldn't have to eat shitty cafeteria food again. Unfortunately, thanks to all the crazy restrictions, no one would let the delivery person up.

"Hey y'all!" A sweet, girl who looked to be barely out of her teens, knocked on the door and then entered the room with what looked like a gift bag in her hand. Immediately, I ran to the other side of the room where my daughter's crib was and grabbed the call button to get a nurse in there.

"Oh, I'm sorry, I didn't mean to startle you. Someone just dropped this off for you at the nurse's desk, but everyone was busy with poor Cody Anderson a few doors down." She poked her lip out in a pout. "She..." She seemed to think better of giving us too much information, but the swipe of the tear running down her cheek said enough. Poor Cody probably didn't make it.

"Texting my dad, that doesn't feel right in combination with the bag being dropped off."

Star was thankfully one step ahead of me, but on the same page. "Can you please, drop the bag and get out?" I asked the girl.

She did as she was told and the nurse who was supposed to be on call for my daughter's room entered. "If you're worried about Lexi, she is supposed to be here. She was vetted by the hospital to work here as a candy striper. It earns her a credit toward..."

"We don't care about Lexi's credits. The girl just delivered a gift bag for my sister that was left at the nurse's station. Do you know anything about it?" Star asked in that no-nonsense way she had of making people get on the right track.

"There wasn't anything left at the nurse's station prior to the code we all just worked."

I walked over to the bag and opened it up, figuring it couldn't be anything that would hurt me, otherwise whoever left it wouldn't have trusted it to do its job after sitting around or being handled by others.

When I got it opened, there was a bloody card sitting on top. *"I'll get her first, but you're next."*

"Oh my God!" I yelled and dropped the bag. The contents rolled out. Besides the threat that had been delivered, there was a babydoll that fell out of the bag. It had been mutilated and stabbed repeatedly. Food coloring or something else was used to simulate the blood coming from each of the stab wounds.

Star didn't waste any more time getting in contact with her dad, Breakneck, and then Bagger who still hadn't come back to the room yet.

"Excuse me!" Someone yelled from the door. "There was a handsome biker in the room with you earlier." The other nurse addressed Star as she spoke.

"Yes, that's right."

"We just found him unconscious on the floor in the bathroom. He's being taken down to the ER for treatment."

Star looked back and forth between the nurse and me. I could see the devastation on her face that she had to make a choice. Stay and help protect me and my daughter or go be beside her man.

"I'll be down as soon as my dad gets here," she finally told the woman.

"Are you sure?"

"Yes, now go!" Star shouted at her before she picked up her cell phone and dialed someone else.

"Scout, tell me they're all on the way!" She paused for a minute obviously listening. "Send them a message. Bagger was injured and left in a bathroom. He's been taken down to the ER. It's just me, Vina, and Coral in the room now. We received a package with a mutilated baby doll inside it and it says: "I'll get her first, but you're next.""

Star listened to Scout speak for a minute or two more and then she nodded her head and hung the phone up. "She's sending more bodies to be able to cover Bagger and both of you."

"I'm so sorry, Star. We will be just fine if you need to go be with him."

"Nope, I would never forgive myself if something happened to either of you. Bagger is a grown man and he's in the crowded ER. He'll be fine. Besides, Kip is going straight for him. Your dad is coming here with Breakneck, and Scout and her friend are already crawling through video to see if they can track down who took Bagger out and left the package."

An hour later, we had our answers.

June and a man who most everyone else seemed to recognize, were in the hospital. They were disguised well. June slipped into the room of Cody Anderson and did something to her that caused the poor girl to code. That was the distraction needed so that the man could slip in behind Bagger and take him out. Then June left the gift bag there for us to find while the two hauled ass out of the hospital again.

Scout and Keys stayed in the room with us working furiously on their respective laptops to find more answers. "Does anyone know this address?" Keys asked. When she read it out, Tripp immediately spoke up.

"That's June's cousin's place. We went there looking for Anna yesterday, but she wasn't there or wasn't answering the door at any rate."

"My girls are here," Keys stated just before we heard a commotion out in the hallway. "Let them know it's okay for them to come back."

Tripp got up and leaned out into the hallway to tell the

nurse to send his sisters back. The nurse rolled her eyes at him but did as he instructed.

"This is JoJo, Christina, and Legs. They're going to stay here with me while you go check out the cousin's place and handle business. I have reason to believe that is where your crazy ex is hiding out." Keys smiled at Tripp. "Don't worry, we'll take good care of your girls while you handle shit. When it's all said and done, the threat will be done for good."

Tripp leaned in, kissed me, and then took off with Mack and Breakneck hot on his heels.

"So, you're all members of a female-only biker club?" They nodded. "That's awesome." I probably sounded like an idiot.

"We think so," JoJo stated. "How are you holding up?"

"I'm just about on my last nerve today, if I'm being honest."

"That's to be expected. I was once in a shootout on the side of a mountain." JoJo confided in me. "It was intense, but my old man was by my side the whole time."

"You obviously made it out."

"We both did."

"Thank you for trying to get my mind off whatever is going on here today, but I don't think it's possible."

JoJo smiled and then gave me a slow nod.

"It was worth a shot." The woman playfully sent me finger guns and a wink before giggling at herself. Under any other circumstances, I could probably be great friends with the women from the S.H.E. MC.

CHAPTER 25
TRIPP

IT WAS a small wonder that no one had called the cops already. Anna's place stunk to high heaven. June's cousin was probably dead before the bitch ever took Barry out. She'd not only killed her cousin brutally but had apparently been living in her place ever since.

"Tripp, you need to see this," Mack stated, and I knew whatever it was would be bad because the man had a cast iron stomach, but looked like he was about to puke.

When I made my way through the only clean spots on the floor to the other room it only took a second for me to find what Mack wanted me to see. There, hung on the wall in the spare bedroom was the picture that a club girl had taken of me and Kim on our last trip to Sturgis. It appeared as though June had tried to desecrate the image. There was a red "X" drawn across Kim's beautiful face, but there was something hanging down from her neck and it looked almost like a cutout doll in a wedding dress had been pasted over the rest of my dead wife's body. When I got closer, I flipped up the sagging bit and found June's face smiling back at me. She had taken her wedding photo, blown it up to match Kim's size in the picture of us, and then taped herself overtop of Kim as if it was some crude wedding portrait for June and me.

"What the absolute nutball shit is that?" Breakneck asked.

"This, the blown-up photo of Kim and me from Sturgis was taken from my house before the fire. That means there's no doubt this bitch killed my wife. This used to hang on our mantel in our house," I informed Breakneck. "I want her in our fucking clubhouse. Find her, man."

Breakneck put his hand on my shoulder in a calming gesture but there wasn't anything that could bring me back from my homicidal state after seeing the evidence that meant I'd entertained dating the woman who killed my fucking wife.

I ripped June's mock wedding photo down and wanted to cry because there were little burn marks and more red exes all over Kim's image. If there had been one thing I missed from that house fire, besides my wife, it was our picture.

"Over here!" Someone shouted. The sounds of a scuffle barely reached my brain as I was stuck somewhere between the past and present and the horrific scene we had to navigate through to find the cunt who had made such a fucking mess of so many lives.

After a minute, Grady and Mack came out with a grinning June in their arms. She fought them until she saw me. "Are you ready to take me back to the clubhouse and make me your old lady?" she asked.

"We're definitely going back to the clubhouse, June."

I turned and walked out while the other men followed quickly on my heels. I looked back at Breakneck then and gave one last order. "Burn it to the ground."

I took a few minutes to myself before I went into the house of horrors. We did not take June back to the clubhouse because she didn't deserve to step foot in our place, not even as a fucking prisoner. Instead, we unanimously decided to take her to the house of horrors where the serial killing bastard who used to rent a room to Kip's nanny had resided. It was luck that between Breakneck and Kip they discovered the conditions that Nova was living in before she became one of the asshole's victims.

"It's fitting that we brought you here," I said to June as they tied her to the rafters in the basement.

"Where are we? This isn't the clubhouse, Tripp. We're supposed to be together now. You need to take me there and give me my patch and your ink. That's what you do, right? That's what Kim told me you did to her."

I stepped forward and backhanded June. "Don't you ever say her name again or I will start keeping count of the teeth I knock out of your mouth. One for every time you dare to spill her name from your vile mouth."

"What the hell are you saying?" June screeched. "You're

mine! Not hers! Never hers! Fuck Kim. Fuck that filthy whore who tried to take you from me."

I struck out faster than even I anticipated and kept my word. A tooth came flying out of June's mouth and thankfully shut her up momentarily. Well, kept her from talking, though she started to cry hysterically.

"Tripp, it's me, June, the love of your life."

"You are nothing to me. I don't even know who the fuck you are. I once dated a girl named June in high school," I mentioned to fuck with her. "She went to Europe on vacation and never came back."

"Yes I did. I'm right here. You never stopped loving me."

"I never loved June. She was just a teenage experiment gone wrong. I've loved two women in my life. One of them was Kim. The other is Davina. I'm not counting my daughters here, obviously since this is the romantic kind of love."

"You don't love those whores. None of them. YOU ARE MINE!" June screamed. I punched her in the mouth again, and true to my word, I knocked another one of her teeth out. She hadn't exactly said my dead wife's name, but she did call both of my old ladies (past and present) a whore.

"Tripp, shtop!" She lisped badly on the last word, and I pretended not to hear her anyway.

"I want to know where your buddy Ken is. If you have any hope of getting out of this basement with any of your teeth left, you need to start talking."

"Ken?" June questioned.

"Kenneth Winslow, otherwise known as Anton Oslav."

"Anton?" she asked, clearly not knowing that the bastard had been going by an alias the entire time she knew him.

"You knew he was into human trafficking, June. You tried to sell my daughter and her friend to him."

She laughed then. "Too bad he never took them as payment. Then maybe your dumbass son wouldn't have knocked that other whore up. Then again, he seems to only have a thing for whores. Like father, like son, Tripp."

I punched her again. "That's three, June. How quickly do you think you'll run out of teeth? Better yet, what do you think I'll start taking away once you run out?"

"You wouldn't. You love me."

I bent down and picked up one of the teeth. "Does this look like I love you?"

"You're just angry. That bitch wife of yours had you brainwashed. We can fix you."

I punched her again. That time, two teeth flew out. They must have all loosened up quite a bit with the previous blows.

"Twipp!" June cried as best she could as blood ran down her chin.

"Tell me where Ken is."

She slumped forward for a minute to spit out more blood. "He's headed to my family's cabin near the Tallulah Gorge."

"On it," Scout called out.

"Keys' people are closer. Want me to have Angel Girl go pick him up?"

"Sure thing. That way we don't have to worry about him slipping through our hands. It'll take too long for us to get there."

I turned back to June. "Now, that wasn't so hard, was it?"

I asked, though I didn't really want an answer. I unsheathed the knife that hung from my belt and held it up in what dim light there was in the basement.

"I wonder how long it will take you to die of sepsis if I give you a bunch of cuts and just leave you to hang here?" I pretended to ponder that for a minute. "Do you think you'd die of dehydration or starvation first?"

"Twipp!" June pleaded.

"Nah, that wouldn't work for me. There would always be a chance that you could escape, and we can't have that." I reached out and sliced one of her arms. I watched as the blood trickled slowly from the wound, down her arm, to the tip of her finger, and then dripped to the ground with the tiniest of noises.

"How are you enjoying your time at the clubhouse, June?" I taunted her. "Too bad you never did fit in there."

"Twipp, no!" She moaned. I sliced her other arm. Before I knew what I was doing, there were superficial wounds up and down her legs and arms. Every inch of skin that was exposed had at least a nick, if not a cut. None of them would kill her, at least not right away. "Do you think my wife felt it when the fire started to consume her?"

"I hope tho," June hissed in her lispy way.

"Mmm, well you'd be disappointed to know that the blow to her head killed her almost instantly and the fire never touched her while she was alive."

"Noo!" June yelled.

"That probably means that you weren't the one who killed her after all."

"Fuck you!" June screamed at me. "I burned her. It was me who did it."

"Nah, you were just the cleanup crew. She was already dead. Your little buddy took that kill from you."

"Noooo! The crazy bitch screamed again.

"Yes!" I informed her gleefully as I stuck the knife into her gut and twisted before bringing it back out. I glanced down and watched her blood and other nastiness fall to the floor. "Oops, looks like I might have perforated your bowels. Guess it won't be long now, but you will suffer before you go, bitch. While you suffer, you're going to watch this little movie Scout made up for you."

When I nodded toward Scout, she used the same projection device we had used in our meeting. This time, she projected some of the home movies and pictures that I still had of my time with Kim and the kids. June screamed and cried through the whole thing and when we ran out of material to play for her, Scout was kind enough to play it all again.

It took five hours for June to die a slow, agonizing death. I stayed for the whole thing. During that time, we got word that Angel Girl and her crew were able to secure Anton Oslav. Since they had been on the lookout for him as well, we sent a member of the club to go oversee his death and disposal.

"I need to get back to my girls," I finally told Mack who stood there staring at what was left of June. He nodded to me and then clapped a hand on my back.

"Hold them tight tonight, Tripp. Don't let this shit drag you into someplace dark."

I shook my head. It was a little too late for that, but I'd

never let the dark shit touch my girls. They were my life now, along with Kip and Knox.

EPILOGUE
TRIPP - 6 MONTHS LATER

"Are you ready, sweetheart?"

"No, my feet are swollen. Do we have to go somewhere?"

I turned to see my gorgeous wife with her pale blonde hair spun up into a bun on top of her head. Her tiny mini me also had a little sprig of hair put up in a cute little bow because she wanted to be so much like her mommy, but she hadn't grown enough hair in yet to make it happen.

Still, they made me smile in their matching dresses. Those were a gift from my oldest daughter, Star, just for this occasion. Not that my girls knew today was a special day.

"Are you sure? I have a special surprise for you both."

Coral started to clap as Vina rolled her eyes. "You spoil us, but seriously, only if it's a short ride because my hips hurt, and my feet really are swollen."

"Okay, sweetheart. I promise, it will be well worth the trip, and I will even massage your feet for you later."

"Massage my feet, you say?"

"Yep. Does that mean you'll get in the truck now?"

"Fine," she sighed. Our daughter mocked her mother and also sighed deeply, as if she knew what was going on. We both chuckled at our little drama queen.

She had been in remission for four months now and had managed to get every bit of sass back she possibly could. It was like she stored it all up with all the napping she had done when sick.

It took less than five minutes to drive to the location we'd picked for our house. We both wanted it to be close to the club, but not too close to town. As soon as we rolled up to the house, Vina looked around. "What are we doing here?"

"Well, that's part of the surprise. I got the boys on the ball and had the house finished ahead of schedule, so we could move in before you pop." I glanced sideways at Vina's growing belly. She was seven months pregnant. Apparently, the first time I was inside her again, I managed to knock her up. The two of us combined were apparently very fertile stock and now, we were two months away from meeting our son. Onyx Perrish Martin. Our boy had also become our daughter's savior, if it was ever necessary. We were having the umbilical cord saved in cryo-storage, because those cells could be used to help Coral if she ever got sick again. Her brother was a very close match to his sister.

"Tripp, we can't just move in. We have to buy furniture and get everything set up. It will probably take me another month to do that. Actually, longer because I can't be on my feet much, since your boy is wearing me out."

"Our boy, and that's okay, sweetheart. Star and Kip managed to get everything set up. They got all the stuff you marked in the catalogs I gave you."

"What?"

"Why don't we get out of the truck and head on inside, so I can show you?"

"Tripp?"

"Yeah, sweetheart?"

"I love you with everything I have."

"Love you even more, sweetheart. Now, let's go home."

When Vina looked up at our house again, Star, Bagger, Kip, Knoxville, and Mr. and Mrs. Avery were all standing there waving at her. A tear rolled down my old lady's face when she noticed them waiting for us.

"I have a home and a family now," she said. It was probably the saddest and most beautiful thing she could have said in that moment, and it only made me love her more.

THANKS FOR READING BABY ME, book #4 in the Savage Vipers MC Series by Anne Storm

Please read/review the book, as this is how other readers find the books you love.

Don't forget to check out the other books in the Savage Vipers MC Series.

- Wait for Me
- Devastate Me
- Surprise Me

WHAT'S NEXT

Patch Me (Savage Vipers MC #5) by Anne Storm

SCOUT

I was a club girl.

What made me different?

They needed me for my skills, and not just the ones that put me on my back to be used.

I never expected the patch.

I fought. I won.

It was mine.

Obtaining it might just cost me the man though.

KIP

After my ex-wife, I swore off women.

I had a son to raise on my own.

Club girls were it for me when I needed to blow off some steam. All of them except the one I really wanted.

Rule number one that my father lived passed down to me: club girls have their place, and it isn't with your patch on their back.

All that changed when she earned her own.

Only, by then, I might have left it too late.

ALSO BY ANNE STORM

ANNE STORM

Savage Vipers MC

Wait For Me · Devastate Me · Surprise Me · Baby Me

Loved for the Holidays

Cupid Broke My Heart · Ghosted by Texas · Resolving Rumors

Cheating Hearts Series

The Homewrecker's Fate · The Regrettable Mistake

Standalone Marriage in Trouble

Nothing Special

CHRISTINE MICHELLE

Kings of Anarchy MC: New Mexico

Property of Bigfoot

Aces High MC – Dakotas

Dancing with Danger · Whiskey Tango Foxtrot · The Restart and the Remedy

Aces High MC – Charleston

The Other Princess · A Love So Hard · The Princess and the Prospect · The Killing Ride · A Twist of Fate · Everlasting · A Year and a Day ·The Broken Beginning – Part One ·The Broken Beginning – Part Two

Aces High MC – Tallahassee

Crushed

Aces High MC – Sierra High

Walker · Trouble

Aces High MC – Cedar Falls

Redemption Weather · Proven · Smoke and the Flame · Redemption Duet Box Set

S.H.E. MC

Angel Girl · JoJo · Keys

Robeson Family Novels (standalones)

The Forgotten Wife · When the Last Petal Falls · A Different Husband

Standalone Novels

The Groupie Journal

Letters to Lily

His Bittersweet Regret

Bad at Love

TFO

The Fortunate Ones

T.I.E. Series

The Infinite Something · The Infinite Beat

Valhalla Rising

Revived

Dark Leopards MC (paranormal)

Ridden by Darkness · The B Team

Mirage Island Mates

Into the Grasslands · Beyond the Grasslands

Seasons Pack Series

Winter Wolves

The Ancients Series

Shadows of the Ancients · Falling into the White · Branches of the Willow · Bound by the Moon

Vukodlak Brew Series

Entwined · Enraged

The Awakening Series

Birthrights · Revelations · Incarnations

Death Viewers

Breathless

Upper YA Titles

The Voodoo Follies (PNR)

Catch a Falling Star (Dystopian Romance)

ABOUT THE AUTHOR

Anne Storm is another pen name for Christine Michelle.
She runs on coffee and giggles as she writes her angst-fueled
romance stories (motorcycle club, rockstar, paranormal,
college, & other contemporary as well as women's fiction
and marriage in trouble novels).
She is a mom to four humans (2 girls, 2 boys – all grown
now).
When she's not writing books, she enjoys reading, drawing,
hiking, or feeding her soul with live music at concerts.
Christine is a traveler and has lived all over the USA (and

other parts of the world). She currently lives in San Antonio, Texas with her two fur babies.

Universal links to everything
(website, social media, book links, and more)
https://linktr.ee/christinemichelle

facebook.com/M00nlitDreams

instagram.com/christinemichelle_annestorm

tiktok.com/@christine.michelle.books